Praise for *A*

"An arcane cosmic horror descends on the day of a heavy metal musician whose own music might just have been the dagger that sliced open the veil between the worlds. Tony McMillen's novel is a love letter pastiche to the occult mythos of rock by way of a mystically-tuned hotel, tentacled horrors, and inter-band relationships, as well as the real-life toll of a debauched life. McMillen's love of music and occulture is infectious. *An Augmented Fourth* has me wanting to search for hidden clues on my old album covers all over again."

—Peter Bebergal, author of *Season of the Witch: How the Occult Saved Rock and Roll*

"Tony McMillen's rock and roll fantasy is a fucking blast. This thinly veiled misadventure combines proto-metal lore with Lovecraftian tradition to birth a heavy hybrid written at maximum volume. Behind the music, in a world much like our own, the devil's chord, church bells, rain, thunder, and weed all coalesce around a hilarious narrative that takes Frivolous Black bassist Codger Burton through withdrawals, cosmic tribulations, metamorphosis, Brummie banter, and world-shaking epiphanies. Tune in, turn on, rock out."

—Nathan Carson, author of *Starr Creek*

"Since *Nefarious Twit*, Tony McMillen has become one of the most unique writers I've read. Over the past weekend I had the great pleasure of cracking his forthcoming, *An Augmented Fourth*—it's metal to the balls *The Thing* meets Black Sabbath riffing Thunderhorse cranked to 11. You guys are in for a treat come June."

—Chris Irvin, author of *Ragged* and *Federales*

"It would take a real virtuoso to properly blend *The Thing, The Mist, Black Sabbath,* and Bowie into one rollicking, comical cosmic horror tribute to early metal and the dark beyond. Lucky for us, Tony McMillen has the chops to make this mutant beast fly on blessed black wings. *An Augmented Fourth* is a strange, sludgy, progged-out blast!"

—Jeremy Robert Johnson, author of *Skullcrack City* and *Entropy in Bloom*

"A ferocious and funny read, full of foot-chases, body horrors, and the requisite screeching monster immolation or two, even some fun wish-fulfillment for connoisseurs of heavy-metal cover art as one of the band's mystery models literally jumps off one of their albums and into the action. [...] To put it all in clearer terms for easier shelving at the video store, think *This Is Spinal Tap* meets *The Thing* meets *From Beyond.* Actually, there wasn't a shelf for the new genre he's conjured up here, but there should have been. In the meantime, I'll be over there waiting for the soundtrack LP so I can scratch it up playing backwards messages."

—David James Keaton, author of *The Last Projector*

An Augmented Fourth

HEY RON,
ENJOY
ONE OF MY
NOVELS ON
THE HOUSE.
THANKS
AGAIN,

TIM MILLER

Other Books by Tony McMillen

Nefarious Twit

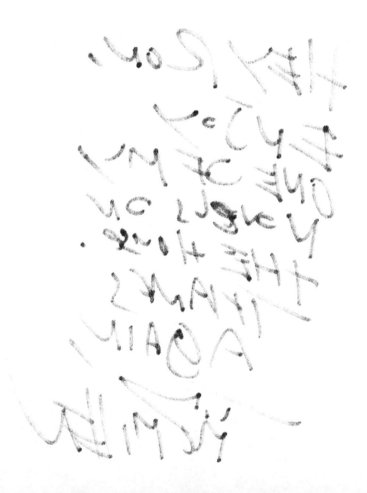

An Augmented Fourth

A Novel of The Lord of Low End

Tony McMillen

WORD HORDE
PETALUMA, CA

First Edition

ISBN 978-1-939905-31-4

A Word Horde Book

To Peter Leon. The first person I remember telling me that a song I wrote was good. And then he told me what was wrong with it. He was right too. Fucker.

Frivolous Black

December 12th, 1980, three days after some Yank shot John Lennon dead on the street in New York City like some unloved dog, and there I was, trapped, snowed in at a hotel in Boston certain that someone was coming to kill me next.

My name's Codger Burton. If you know me it's because I'm the bass player for the heavy metal band Frivolous Black. But you probably don't know me.

I'm the bass player.

I also wrote most of the band's lyrics but some fucker with a high-pitched voice got to sing them so he gets most of the credit. I don't mind that. Most of the best things I ever wrote felt like they were written by somebody else anyways. Which makes it a bit weird to take much credit. If somebody asked me where'd I come up with the words to "Beyond This Sleepless Dream" or "Tetrahex" or any of the old stuff, I wouldn't know what to tell them. Except it's almost like they were given to me. Just waiting out there for someone, anyone, to grab them. Like somebody else would have written them eventually if I hadn't have been the one. But I was. That's the whole problem I suppose.

I don't know how long I was unconscious in my hotel room but when I came to the first thing I did was stumble-step to the window, part the blinds, and look out at the endless white swirling outside. The storm didn't notice me back. The whole city was covered in snow, the taller buildings looked like massive, gleaming white bone, newly cleaned and jutting out of the earth. I watched, silently mesmerized as more and more perfect white flakes fell down playfully all over the cold dead city.

Fuck me, this was going to be a shit time to try and kick cocaine.

We were touring behind our new record with our new frontman and trying to restart the band's career when I decided to restart myself and finally give up the coke and the drink and all (most) of the other assorted bullshit. I suppose all the rest wasn't a big enough challenge. Quitting cocaine isn't like kicking heroin, or so I've been told. You don't puke and thrash about or any of that, it's more like the biggest comedown you've ever had, but Christ help you do you crave more coke. Quitting booze on the other hand, there was plenty of puking and shaking to go along with that. Feeling like my skin was falling off of my body in hot wet sheets one minute and then that stabbing deep cold that had me churning like a dead leaf in a breeze the next. Shit, I might as well have done the smack with the state I was in now. There's a song off our second album, the one everybody owns, about heroin addiction. I wrote it after all these Yank soldiers coming back from Vietnam started turning up at some of our early gigs in England. They had seen and done so many fucked things over there that they had all started shooting up to deal with it. There were practically piles of syringes covering the ground at some of the shows after everyone had left. Poor bastards, they were just trying to get away from their own private hell but instead ended up inviting it back straight into their veins. I could relate in a small way. I guess we all can.

My own hell wasn't so bad really, especially in comparison. It's hard to moan about being rich and famous and getting to do what I love for a living but of course I still manage. My own hell was called Frivolous Black and I had spent eleven years in it at that point. From back when we were a blues group called Soil 'til the day Vinnie came in to band practice with a new direction and a new kind of riff, saying maybe we should be playing "doomy tunes," right up until we sacked our frontman, Sully Sullivan, last year. I've been there for it all. And some of it has been good, very good. Heaven even. But of course that just makes the other side even worse. And if you're looking at your old LPs and wondering which one I am, of the three gentlemen with long hair and drooping moustaches standing with their arms folded behind our clean-shaven, oddly angelic looking lead singer, I'm the one with the bushiest hair and the second-best moustache.

Now Frivolous were touring behind our new record with our new lead singer, a Yank, no moustache either (I don't think lead singers are allowed to have them for some reason) and we were almost done with this leg of the tour. Just one more gig here in Boston at the Boston Garden, then a nice big break for Christmas and New Year's so I could go back to Birmingham and maybe see my relations. Of course that last gig was supposed to be today, but the entire city was practically shut down due to the snowstorm from what the television said yesterday, so needless to say our concert was cancelled too. It pained me to give the parasite any credit at all, but when our road manager, Peter Dorsbry, got word of how shit the weather was suspected to turn in our area he had all of us switch hotels. 'Least that's what he told me on the phone when he called me five hours ago incredulous that I hadn't been swept up with the rest of the band, the roadies, our trusted dealers, birds and various other muckers and barnacles that had attached themselves to the great underbelly of the Frivolous organization over the last ten years, ever since the band trundled its way out of Birmingham.

"You're still there at the Hotel Alucinari? Codger, Jesus, man. You're snowed in, you know? Nobody can get to you until maybe tomorrow. You know I had your room searched? Nobody saw you. Where were you hiding, might I ask?"

That conversation with Peter was before my moment at the window looking out at the white skeleton city. When I woke up later I thought I had left the window open it was so cold, which is why I walked up to it. But it was still sealed, which meant the heat had been turned off. I checked the phone and it was dead too. TV and lights the same. They had shut the power off after they evacuated the building, or maybe the storm had knocked it out. I didn't even have a watch to tell what bloody time it was. Brilliant. Luckily I had an even worse problem to occupy my mind: The absolute center of my head felt like it was caving in at that moment. I remember getting sick and going to the toilet before finally passing out again.

When I woke up, I was in the closet for some reason, not laying down on the floor but standing straight up like a vampire's prick in his crypt. I didn't know how much time had passed, but sunlight was still creeping in through the window so it couldn't have been too long. I was getting the shakes pretty bad at this point and I just wanted to find somewhere dark and quiet. So I went to the toilet where I could return to being sick. I always had a fragile stomach. Sully used to stand over me while I let it loose and clap his hands and laugh. He'd call it my "solo project." Bastard. His actual solo project was going along swimmingly, that first single with his new guitar player, fucking bostin'. Even though that fucker was a Yank, Christ could he could play... When I closed my eyes it felt like my brain was swelling up against the inside of my skull like some hot air balloon made of meat. The fucking drink. I had been hitting it too hard for years, I knew that, but we had all been hitting it hard. Why did I choose now to try and kick it along with the coke? I was setting myself up to fail all over again. I had gotten sober for five months a year ago when we fired Sully. It didn't feel right throwing him out of the band for being a coked out alcoholic loon when the rest of us were also coked out alcoholic loons. So I quit drinking and the coke then, just to be sanctimonious, which was the second time I tried to quit and the first time it stuck. Well, stuck for five months. It had been bad then, really bad. But now was worse. No matter how many times I think I've turned my back on the church, when I'm puking, I'm a believer. No one's an atheist when they're hungover. Hell, when you're trying to kick you might as well be born again. Believe me.

I think I may have been getting the DTs then, because in the bathroom on my knees, face hovering above the toilet bowl full of my own sick, looking perversely like I worshiped the filth that my body produced, I kept thinking I could see something black swarming in the corners of my eyes. Some flickering, weird, unexpected crackle like when you opened a sugar jar only to find a vortex of shiny black ants crisscrossing in and out of the white granulated dust...

Christ, I needed some coke. I thought, *maybe I should just quit the drink but keep the coke for a bit. Maybe just 'til I'm off the bottle...*

I waited for about ten minutes and when I didn't puke again I got slowly to my feet.

This was day two off any shit and I knew it could get bad again but I also got the sense that a relief period was coming. I went to the mirror out of habit but avoided looking at myself in the eye like it was a divine mandate. Of course curiosity got the better of me, like it usually did, and I gave myself a quick appraisal: My eyes looked like an empty auditorium. The skin on my face was taut and greasy and there were bruised, almost green circles forming around my eyes. On top of that, even my moustache looked shit. Maybe I always looked this bad and now I was just sober enough to see it. Then that black flicker again off to the sides of my vision, dark tiny tadpoles dancing in my peripheral. I had the distinct sensation of the gnarled tips of black tree branches curling around my head then receding swiftly from my view. I turned around stupidly to investigate and of course there was nothing. Fucking DTs. I needed something to do before I started seeing little green men coming out of the upholstery. So after procuring a pair of pants from my luggage and putting on my complimentary bathrobe, I left my room in hopes of finding something, anything, to get my mind off of things. Before I left the room I looked back at the window, watched the storm for a bit more, the snow corkscrewing through the air this way and that. Everything inside the room with me then was still and quiet and the only sound in the whole world was the long sustained howl of the wind outside.

Hotels mostly look the same on the inside. I've been living in them for the last decade, and the Hotel Alucinari was no different than any of the rest but still, I'd never been in an abandoned hotel before. I'd stayed in the Alucinari a few times in the past, the place saw a lot of traffic from people in my line of work. It was no Hyatt House or Chelsea Hotel but it was the closest equivalent that Boston could muster. I even heard that Frankie Gideon, who was supposed to play the Garden the night after us, was staying here too.

From the outside the hotel looked like someone had made a Middle Ages Catholic Church from an antique hypodermic syringe, but once you were inside the Alucinari was as ordinary as any other hotel. But now that the power was out some of the mystique that the exterior had conjured for me had returned. I flicked open my Zippo to see where I was stepping in the dark halls, and where I was stepping was onto a weird, red and dark brown American Indian looking pattern on the carpet. The halls were even quieter than I expected. It lent the place a seriousness that bordered on reverence. I suppose I should have found the whole thing terribly creepy or frightening, especially after seeing that film about the haunted hotel and the little lad on the tricycle going up and down the halls while that crazy fucker from *Chinatown* with the eyebrows went all yampy and ran around with an axe, but I wasn't scared. Not yet. After being in the Satan-courting, evil incarnate outfit known as Frivolous Black for so long, I just found most of that spookshow stuff boring now. When you're in the band that supposedly created heavy metal, and you wear black to work every day and go on stage and play songs about the devil and the atrocities of the human condition to thousands of doomed-out, bong-brained teenagers, it kind of ruins haunted houses for you. Halloween too. Having Anton LaVey at our album release party would have ruined Satanism for me too, but I was never really too keen on the idea to begin with. Seems like a bunch of atheists with a sense of pageantry if you ask me. Don't tell the press that though, it'd ruin our mystique. That is, if our new album and new singer didn't do that already.

The guy was a Yank for starters. And maybe the whole thing with Lennon had got me prejudiced as of late, but I spent the last three days watching TV and feeling like the world was ending; crying while I watched the news, realizing that whatever the dream of the 60s and my youth was, it was never coming back. Lennon was dead. It was over. That's where my head was at. And besides, it just felt weird having a Yank singing in Frivolous.

Don't tell Vinnie, but it felt weird having anyone but Sully singing, if I'm being totally honest. But this new guy being a Yank felt doubly wrong. And secondly, this pleb wrote his own lyrics, which was fine with me because I was struggling for material to give to Sully for the last couple of records anyway, but the trite, superficially Satanic wizards and warlocks horseshit that this bloke came up with... it was pedestrian. It was unreal how beneath us it was. The worst part was that I knew what he was trying to do... and I almost understood why.

He was trying to capture that dark occult thing that we did on the first three Frivolous records. Because they're easily the most popular records. They're the ones that everyone knows us for. That's how they remember us no matter how much we grow out of it. They want songs about the devil or about strange, otherworldly sinister forces, songs about madness, about surrendering to the darkness inside and fighting against the darkness out. I don't know what they want actually, I never did. But they want what we did, what we used to do... effortlessly. Because those songs happened organically. That's what this Yank didn't realize. That's what Vinnie, our guitarist, and Burt, our drummer, don't remember: We didn't set out to invent heavy metal or to make horror music, it just happened. Back in those days we would just show up to our practice space or a recording room and it was like the songs were already written. Like they were given to us from somewhere else. We used to joke that it was our secret fifth member. Our Brian Wilson, transmitting his demos to us from somewhere in hell. The music felt natural even if it was unlike anything we'd ever heard before. It wasn't contrived, it wasn't assembly-lined, it didn't try to sound scary. It just was. The scariest thing of all was just how good it was. But now, with this new album and this new singer, we sounded like all those other bands full of half-soaked geezers that tried to sound like us and failed.

I moved through the hall slowly waving my Zippo flame, half pretending I was exploring some desolate old cavern or something. I always had a healthy imagination. I wasn't hungry exactly but I could eat and I could also use a smoke. The scariest part of this whole snowed in-abandoned hotel experience so far had been when I realized I already smoked my last cigarette. I made a silent prayer (possibly to the toilet god I had left back in my room) that I'd find a working cigarette machine or a mummified former cave explorer with my brand in his cobwebbed pocket somewhere in the lobby.

Of course without electricity the lifts were dead, so I walked past their useless doors and was about to proceed down the hall to the stairs when out of the dark to my left a burning hand appeared. I froze, stifled a scream, then craned my head to the side and found my reflection studying me. It was the long rounded mirror situated between the lifts. There floating in the dark it looked like some sort of bubble with a man inside it. He looked scared and when he laughed at himself for being so barmy and stupid he just looked old and scared. I left him there in his bubble and decided to take the stairs down.

I was only on the fourth floor so it wouldn't be that much of a descent. Pale blue light shot in from long rectangular windows lining the far right wall of the stairwell, and I had to pass through the little rivers of light with each floor I traveled. As I neared the bottom the wind outside started picking up into a din that the stairwell amplified. This place got a pretty good sound actually. Could be a good place to record drums. Big, fuck a mountain into rubble sort of sound, like Friv got on our fifth record. We recorded that at a bleeding castle, it was miserable. Better than when we recorded the next one in Florida though. We shared a studio with the fucking Eagles and before we could record anything properly we'd have to scrape all their cocaine out of our mixing board. Must have been a pound of that shit left on the board. Good shit too. Waste not, want not. The Eagles… they'd do that and then bellyache about us playing too loud next door and they had to keep stopping while they were trying to record "Hotel Fucking California." The sound we made was bleeding through the walls. Too bad we couldn't get them to just call it a day and stop recording that awful dreck altogether. Believe me, we did try.

At some point the storm outside stopped sounding like one lone voice to me and instead turned into a choir of howling, untethered singing. Part of me wished to stay there on that stairwell letting the sound fall down and wash over me. The sound was dissonant, yes, but it was agreeably dissonant. Like waking up on a beach hearing the ocean's murmur. Part of me could listen to that racket forever. But the other part still wanted its smokes.

I walked across the marble tile floor of the lobby, ignoring everything but the cluster of vending machines sitting beneath a massive mural of some sort of battle, a typical Yank celebration of death and war. The lobby was dimly lit from the large glass windows that covered most of the walls. The windows were choked with snow from bottom to top but a weak amount of sunlight could still be seen sneaking its way in here and there, and that and my Zippo gave me a pretty good look at the mural. Not that I cared enough to give it a proper study, I just wanted my smokes. There was a candy machine, a fizzy pop machine, and finally, oh yes, a cigarette dispenser. And wonder upon wonders they had my brand, Cherry Valleys!

Then I reached into my pocket and found absolutely no money. In fact there was nothing in my pocket except for two guitar picks. Not even a lighter or a book of matches—I grinned, what a half-soaked fool I could be, I still had the lit Zippo in my hand for Christsake. And money wasn't going to be a problem either obviously. I walked across the floor, the air in the center of the room felt especially cold, and I picked up the second smallest potted plant I could find, walked back and threw it into the cigarette dispenser. The dispenser was hard plastic and it did not break, merely cracked. I dropped the plant after three or four more vigorous attempts, then walked over to its larger compatriots. I was about to lift up one of the heavier ones when I saw the familiar red outline of an emergency box hung along the wall behind the miniature jungle I was set to uproot. I took the smallest plant in my arms and used it to break the glass, then I took out the axe. The axe made short work of the vending machine plastic after only a few well-coordinated thwacks. I was always pretty good with an axe. There was this one time on the road, six or seven years ago, when me and Sully got a right cob on and took a couple axes to Burt's hotel room while he was god knows where. We weren't in a row with Burt, not at all, we just were in the mood, had the axes for some reason, and were in Burt's room at the time. Getting an axe stuck in a box spring mattress is a real drag when you're in the midst of a proper man tantrum. Watching Sully Sullivan light said box spring on fire in subsequent frustration, however, is an indelible pleasure that made it all worthwhile.

As I brushed away the plastic and picked up my pack of Cherry Valleys I found myself staring up at the Yank mural. A bunch of Bostonian Yanks butchering some of my countrymen with muskets over some land they both stole from the red man. Typical hypocrite Yank statement. At least in England we know we're fucking awful. I left the mural and had already popped a fag in my mouth and lit it when another craving made itself known: hunger. I went to the front desk to search for complimentary mints, or maybe some chocolates if they had them, and found some peppermints in a large oblong bowl next to the bell. A tent card behind the bowl suggested, *only take one please*, but I thought better of it and took a handful.

"What are you doing here?" The voice came from behind me, it was thin sounding, young, masculine but not yet a man, sort of squawky like a bird trying to sound bigger than it really was… American. I turned around to see a teenage boy in a bellhop uniform brandishing a flashlight like it was some sort of weapon. Which it was, I supposed since it hurt my damn eyes. His bellhop hat was askew on his head, betraying his long black hair which sprawled out well past his shoulders. Even in the dimly lit room I could see how greasy and acne-scarred his thin oval face was. When he opened his mouth again I saw the unmistakable glint of metal braces. "…You're Codger Burton." The bird didn't sound so big then. And I thought I detected a faint trace of accent to his voice then. Mexican perhaps? "What are you doing here? I mean, I knew you were here but what are you *still* doing here?" The question I've been asking myself as of late. He lowered the flashlight from my face, baring his metal as his mouth hung open.

"I must have slept through the evacuation." I removed a mint from its wrapper and popped it in my mouth then took a short drag, letting the good thick smoke coat my bile-cut throat. "I will say that I'm surprised a place like this would hire someone like you who knows something like that."

"Like what?"

"Like my name and who I am."

I think he blinked a total of seven times before his computation was complete and he could respond. "...I know, right? It's not a bad job except that they make me wear a fucking ponytail. I look like a total pussy but I gotta work, at least that's what my mom says. Oh man, Codger Burton! Check this out." He lifted up his shirt before I could persuade him not to. Instead of the skinny zit-covered torso I expected to see, he was wearing a t-shirt underneath his uniform. Of course it was a Frivolous Black one; not a tour shirt I noted, it was the cover to *Schizoid*, the second album. The one everyone owns. The kid was pointing at his shirt in case I missed it and smiling with that metal shit all over his teeth the whole time. I hated this kid. His stupid fucking face, his stupid fucking shirt that had my stupid fucking band name on it. Then he said, "You're my favorite lyricist and third favorite bass player..." At least he was being honest. "Frivolous Black is the entire reason I exist, man, it totally gives my life purpose!" Then his face dropped a little. "But I gotta say, that new singer guy fucking sucks, man. No disrespect, but without Sully and your words it doesn't sound the same. When are you gonna fire that assleak and get Sully back in the band?"

I liked this kid.

"Also, it'd be an honor to smoke a bowl with the man who wrote 'Hazel Daze.' You want to toke up?"

I really liked this kid.

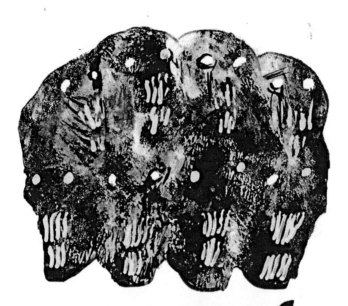

FRIVOLOUS BLACK

THE NEW ALBUM

"SCHIZOID"

OPTIKOS
RECORDS

Hazel Daze

The kid's weed was complete shit. But I didn't tell him that. I smoked worse when I was his age. In between puffs he told me his name was John. John Lopez. I think he said he was seventeen but he looked closer to sixteen to my eyes. Not that I was paying too much attention to him. The weed may have been shit but dear Christ did I need it. The withdrawals were still eating away at me terribly. The kid asked me if I had looked outside, *did I know what was out there?* How bad it had gotten… etc. I told him yeah, yeah, I knew all about the snowstorm, that we were probably stuck in here. He told me there was no probably about it. The kid waited about four tokes before he asked his first real question, "So… Mr. Burton, like, how did you guys make the first two albums so fast? I read it was like five days for *Schizoid* and only one day for the debut. How is that even, like, possible?"

I took my drag; I've been answering Frivolous questions since I can remember. The same Frivolous questions too. I cashed the bowl. But… this kid was nice. "That's right, mostly. The second album took a week but the self-titled was more like a day and a half. The recording was done in a day but the mixing was all done the next and I think that's when we over-dubbed the rainstorm and bell sound effects and all that other nonsense." I handed him his pipe. "We out?" He nodded. "You know where to get us a bite?"

"…Huh?"

"Some fittle." He looked at me like I was speaking bloody Japanese. And even though I hadn't really expected him to understand me, my tone was curt. "Some food, man… Jesus."

"I don't really know… actually there might be some food up in one of the supply closets."

"Supply closet? What, next to the mops and the chemicals and shit?"

"Yeah, like sometimes the maids store snacks and whatnot in there."

This kid. "Are you going fucking yampy on me? Where's the kitchen, man?"

"You want to go to the kitchen?"

"That's generally where food is found, is it not?" The kid nodded. "Then how about we go there?"

"You know the supply closet… I'm pretty sure I saw some crackers in there—"

"'Crackers' he says? How high are you, kid? The supply closet is up them stairs, right?" He nodded again, a bit reluctantly I noted. "If this hotel is anything like all the other bleeding hotels I've been to, which it is because I'm an expert and they're all the fucking same, that means that the kitchen is on the ground floor. Which we're on, right? And they must have a fair amount more than some old lady's stale crackers what have bleach spilled on them at the very least, right?"

His shoulders sank, poor kid, not only was he too high to make any decent decisions, his hero was turning out to be a right prick. "Yeah, I guess."

"You know what the Latin word for old lady is?"

"No."

"Anus. It is anus."

"…Oh, I thought anus came from the word for like, a ring?" He made a little circle with his finger in the air.

The kid might have perked up an ear in school occasionally through his bong fog. "Fine, they're two different words, a-nus and ah-nus, but they're spelled the same."

"…Okay."

"So let's pass on the anus crackers shall we? Right, to the kitchen then please, thank you."

The kid led us with his flashlight to the kitchen, said there should be plenty there for me to gnaw on. He never took his eyes off me. I thought he was going to walk right into a wall at least twice as we made our way to this kitchen. "So, like, on 'Tetrahex,' on the intro, that's all you on the bass with the wah-wah, right? Like, even though it sounds like it might be Vinnie's guitar it's really just you, right?" He basically didn't really want or need to learn anything. He already knew it all. He just wanted to hear me say it. He wanted to hear it repeated back to him.

"Yeah, that's just me." We took a corner, the kid trailed me like some starving puppy dog.

"How did you think of the words for 'Visitation Rites'?"

"I don't know, I just heard the riff that Vinnie had and then the melody that Sully came up with and when me and Burt figured out the rhythm section the words just sort of came to me."

"Just like popped into your brain out of nowhere?"

"No…" My brain felt like it was pressing against the inside of my skull trying to break out, maybe the kid's weed was better than I gave it credit for. "More like the words were waiting underneath some sort of overgrowth or a thick skin, and all that had to be cleared away bit by bit until I could see what I was supposed to see there. Like it was waiting patiently for me to discover it."

"…That's exactly how it is for me, like, when I write my songs too!" Of course it was. But I could tell where this was going because it always went there eventually. These kinds of fans, these young guys—always young guys, never ever a good-looking woman with a head on her shoulders—these boys, they always wanted to ask the one question. All the rest is just preamble. Them working up the guts to ask it. The kid opened his mouth, the silver in his smile flashed, and I knew it was coming: "So, like, Mr. Burton, when you guys wrote the first song, 'Frivolous Black,' the song itself, I heard… I mean, I read, the whole thing was about a real thing that happened to you. The black shape that appeared at the foot of your bed… the visitation and the Aleister Crowley book… is all of that true?"

Just past him I could see the door marked Kitchen. I thought back to one cold night in Birmingham and what had happened to me there, how I lied about it ever since. How that lie changed my entire life. How I'd never tell anyone the truth. Not the whole truth. So I told the kid, "Not a word of it. That whole deal with the devil, sold my soul for rock and roll; complete and utter bullshit I'm afraid." The kid lost his smile and I walked past him and headed into the kitchen.

Inside I could still smell the ghosts of a thousand old feasts hanging in the air. Most recently some roasted chicken or possibly pheasant. It smelled good, actually it smelled delicious. Very delicious. I was starving. The kid put his flashlight down on one of the long silver prep tables. "There's usually leftovers and prep stuff in the walk-in fridge," he told me. "The power's off but it's so cold everything has probably kept," he added. I didn't care if the meat in there had portabellas growing out of it; I would eat any goddamn thing. "Just wait here and I'll get you something." He came back with some cold but already cooked fried chicken. He put the plate down on the table near the flashlight and I snatched a drumstick and tore into it instantly. I didn't know the last time I had anything to eat; I could only remember things coming out of my mouth in the opposite direction.

"Why are you still here, kid?" The meat was cold but not frozen. I stripped all the flesh from the bone and moved on to the next piece.

"You want me to… leave while you eat?"

I laughed. "No, no, I'm asking why you stayed back in this hotel after they cleared the place out. I told you my excuse, what's yours?"

He was standing just behind the beam of the flashlight which covered the wall to his right. His features were mostly hidden and his eyes, barely glints. "I… I knew you were staying here actually. At least there was a rumor you were staying here, the whole band. That's why I got the job, a lot of bands coming through Boston stay here at the Alucinari. I got to meet the guys from Red Horse in July. Frankie Gideon is staying here right now too, but I don't really listen to that fruity shit."

"Gideon is a legend. You Yanks are always five years behind, in half a decade you'll be wearing his t-shirt." I looked up from my chicken. "So you stayed here in hopes that I was left behind?" Flashes of Lennon on the street went through my mind.

"What? No." He shrugged his shoulders. He was either working out a story or working up the courage to come clean. I wanted to see his face better. Wanted to know how close any knives in this kitchen might be. "I… thought that since you and Friv might have been here I would check out your rooms… see if you left anything behind." Was that it? He was looking for a keepsake?

"You were hoping for a fucking guitar pick?"

"That'd be cool… some drugs would also be nice."

"What makes you think I or any other musician would leave something as valuable as drugs behind whilst fleeing a hotel in the middle of a city as culturally stimulating as Boston, U.S.A?"

"…Dude, I know, but people were leaving in a hurry. I already scored like fifty bucks and a pair of panties and I've only searched ten rooms."

This fucking kid.

"You didn't even know what rooms we were staying in?" I finished my drumstick, then took another piece of chicken. Wasn't sure what to make of his story, maybe I should ask to see the panties? "What else you got in that fridge? If you have any mash I'll take that if you don't mind."

"Cold?"

"Nothing wrong with a bit of cold mash. Used to eat it like that all the time." Kid responded with a little smile that looked sort of sinister with the lighting and then he went to looking for what I'd asked. Kid wouldn't be a half bad roadie actually. As long as he wasn't another psycho killer like the fucker who shot Lennon. I was about to inform him of this fact, subtracting the Lennon murderer bit, to give him a little something to make up for letting him down outside the kitchen just now, when we heard screaming. It was coming from outside the kitchen walls. It happened again. Louder. It wasn't quite clear if it was a man or a woman's voice; it sounded human, but that's all I could discern. Part of me wondered, almost wanted to delude myself, that there was no scream. That it was just the storm outside really letting it rip. But then we heard it again. No mistaking that, it wasn't coming from the outside, it was in the hotel here with us.

"Is anyone here with you?" the kid asked.

"No, you?"

He shook his head. "Should we… like, investigate?"

I took another bite of chicken. "Yes, I suppose we should," I told him through the mouthful.

I took a couple of wings for the road and we made it out into the hall to complete quiet. No more screams, even the storm seemed to be resting. I was ready to propose we get back to the kitchen and get to finding that mash when the stop-start staccato of heeled footsteps came clicking and clacking in from the marble floor just around the corner. The sound started getting louder, faster. Then I realized it wasn't one pair of footsteps. Behind the heeled shoes or boots there was another pair of feet. They sounded louder, deeper but not as rushed. But they were following the first pair, of that much I was certain. We kept moving away from the kitchen, the kid in front with his flashlight. With the sound bouncing off the walls and everything else bouncing off my skull in my current state, it was hard for me to determine which direction the steps were coming from. I looked to the right then to the left. There was a corner in either direction, maybe about twenty or thirty feet away, give or take, from where we were standing. But even as the steps neared the corner the heavier ones in pursuit never sped up. And still, the screaming had stopped.

I made a guess that the footsteps were coming from the right corner. I looked at the kid and he had his flashlight at the ready like it was a service revolver… fucking Americans. For my part, I took the smallest bite of chicken wing I could manage and still be coherent if conversation threatened to conjure itself. Footsteps were even louder now. But nothing was in front of me. Then the sound was around the corner, the left corner; fuck me and my certainties. Running around the left corner to face us was something more terrifying than I could have possibly expected: a punk rocker.

I recognized her right off, Rikki Spectre of Rikki and the fucking Spectres.

Expletive mine, not the actual band name. The arty-fartsy half English, half Somali punker who wore too-goddamn-much eyeliner, with hair like a dying black bird, she had practically made an art form out of not smiling. Why was Rikki fucking Spectre terrifying to someone like me? Because Rikki fucking Spectre's entire existence was just further proof that me and my band were relics. Our time was up. Sure, we're still selling tickets, people were still buying LPs even with that goddamn American dwarf handling the singing chores, but we were no longer relevant. Punk killed that. Punk had killed metal. At least that's how it appeared then. And Rikki was terrifying to me because her band actually could play. They wrote some good tunes, she had a voice, something to say with it. And worst of all, I could tell all this, that she was important and that she spoke for and to the youth, but I also realized that I could not relate to her and her music at all. I was out of the circle. I was an old, out of touch millionaire recreating and pantomiming his glory days on stage to arenas full of less successful, still aging burnouts doing the same.

I was aware then of how hilarious it was that someone who willingly calls himself Codger was complaining about feeling old all of a sudden. I was also aware that I was only thirty-five then in that hotel as I was feeling like a has-been, but we lived fast in Frivolous. Rock and roll in general, everything is accelerated but also elongated. Like how your childhood years felt like decades were crammed into them. That's how it felt being in a band, making albums, touring. You live so much, learn so much, change so much, do so much in such little time. I think the common denominator in both childhood and rockstardom is relentless change, growth. The monotony of most people's lives makes every day, every year, feel like one big endless drone. Time stretches on and on, with no distinction and therefore no form, no order. But with living on the road, like childhood, the years feel longer but they also go by quicker too. Before you know it, there's some kid like Rikki fucking Spectre running around and turning corners, reminding you how much of a fucking ghost you've become.

So obviously I pretended I didn't know who she was when I saw her. "What's the rush? Are you being followed, miss?"

"Is that... whoa, shit it is... Rikki Spectre!"

This fucking kid.

"I don't know if I'm being followed but who you calling 'Miss'?" Chislehurst, southeast London, rich parents. Nearly as bad as a Yank.

"Look here, nothing was meant by it, now will you tell us why you're running around this hotel?" I asked her, and halfway through I tried my best not to sound like her father reprimanding after a late night with no call.

"I'm running because I saw something weird and I thought the best course of action, seeing as I'm snowed in to this hotel, was to run the hell away from it."

"What did you see, was it a ghost?" the kid asked.

"What, so the hotel is haunted then?" I asked.

He shrugged one shoulder. "I don't know. It's just, like, the first thing I thought of."

"No, I didn't see a ghost. I just saw something... it must have been... well, I don't know what it was but it's not a fucking ghost."

I took another bite of chicken before I realized it and then remembered the other pair of footsteps, the heavier ones. They were still coming, only now much slower. They heard us, whoever it was could hear us, and they were slowing their approach. The low sound of them was coming from the other corner. We all seemed to hear it and went quiet. I looked to Rikki and she shook her head and held her hands up. I had a large bite of chicken in my mouth and what scared me the most was accidently choking on it when mister big boots came around the corner to say howdy. Things like that happen to me all the time; inopportune bodily processes. Like when you're holding in a fart because someone else is telling you something important, like that they want a divorce. I managed to chew my chicken slowly, braced myself for whatever was around the bend. A man walked out, an ordinary man holding a flashlight. He was terrifically tall, barrel-chested with a wonderful round bulb of Afro on his head and a ridiculously thick winter coat on. His name was Marcus Wilkes and I kind of knew him. He was a Vietnam vet turned bodyguard, specializing in rock stars with drinking problems, sort of a responsible enabler. He used to babysit Jim Morrison until the Lizard King absconded to Paris and sent word that he wouldn't require Marcus' services anymore. He was dead five months later. Too bad John Lennon hadn't had him on the payroll three days ago, eh? We wanted to hire him to take care of Sully a few years ago but Marcus was committed to his current gig, the glam vamp Frankie Gideon. And that was sure to be a full time engagement. Frankie was the only one I'd ever seen keep pace with Sully when it came to nostril coca-cola. "Marcus, what are you doing here?"

"Have any of you seen Frankie?" He looked worried; I'd never seen him even look annoyed before. Even with the lunatics he wrangled for a living. "I'm looking for him. I was on the phone with the road manager when the power went out and he was saying that Frankie didn't leave with the rest of the band or crew when they got out."

"Why didn't you leave with everybody else in the first place?"

My paranoia was getting the best of me, I was suspecting even rock star bodyguards.

"I stayed back to make sure he wasn't here, after I couldn't find him I gave the road manager a call," Marcus said. He made it fairly obvious that he didn't like being questioned.

"I haven't seen you and I've been looking around the hotel for a while," the kid said without malice or accusation. More like he was just stating a surprising fact.

"Maybe you didn't see me, maybe I did see you... has anybody seen my client?"

"Um," Rikki said. She had somehow found the time to light a cigarette. Not Cherry Valleys, by the by. "That's kind of what I was running from."

I swallowed my chicken. "What?"

Heathen's Greetings

"I saw Frankie in a lift, he was going down," Rikki said.

"That's surprising then, isn't it?" I said to no one in particular.

"Smartass," Rikki said.

"I'm not trying to insult the man but how the hell could he take the lift when the power's out then?"

"The power's out?" she asked.

"Why the fuck do you think we're in the dark?" I told her.

"I just woke up not more than fifteen, twenty minutes ago, I didn't know, excuse me."

"You guys sure do sleep through things," the kid said.

"When did you see Frankie, just now?" Marcus asked.

"It was about ten minutes ago or so."

"And that's why you were running? That's what got you screaming? Frankie in the lift?" I dropped my chicken bones on the floor. If it bothered the kid he didn't let me know.

"I wasn't the one screaming." She said that and only that. Who the hell says something like that without following it up with the identity of the actual screamer? The pain in my head had shifted. Not left, just shifted. The dull pierce had given way to a sort of steady pressure. Right in the center of my skull. When I closed my eyes flashes of deep swamp blue and dark reptilian green washed over. And again, the image

29

of black branches retreating back into the dark. I felt like my brain was submerged in tar, that it was filling, swishing this way and that just behind my eyes. I needed to sit down or else I was going to be sick again.

But instead I said, "Who was screaming then?"

"Frankie?" Marcus asked.

"…I don't know." The ember from her cigarette flashed orange. "He wasn't alone."

"What do you mean?" The kid entered the conversation.

"It's going to sound stupid when you hear it."

"That hasn't stopped you yet." I said it and immediately regretted it.

"What's that supposed to mean?"

"This whole punker attitude you're affecting with the 'don't call me "Miss"' business and what all."

"'Affecting,' he says? Listen here, you old dried up, bullshit macho, heavy metal fossil, that is if you can understand basic human language through the fog of your dope and booze cocoon—"

"'Dried up'? What have you achieved? You've made one damn record so far."

"Oh, so you've heard it then?"

"Yeah, I have. Not bad but you know what? It's been almost two years since you put it out."

"So?"

"So, back when I was your age Friv was putting out two a year. What's the matter, dear, you and yours already run out of ideas?"

"Fuck you."

"I was just talking a bit of shit just then, but now I think I might have actually hit the nerve. Maybe you're the one who's dried up?"

"Fucking wank—"

"Cut the shit," Marcus said. "You were telling a story, you mind getting back to telling it?"

"Fine. I had woken up, realized the phone wasn't working, didn't jump to the conclusion that the power was out too, god forbid. Did however jump to the conclusion that the hotel had been evacuated because I heard rumblings about it being a possibility last night, and finally I figured out that my fucking band and our people had forgotten and left me behind despite being the band's fucking namesake." She flashed her cat eyes at me. "So, I was walking around the Alucinari, trying to make the most of it, maybe find something to eat..." I offered her a chicken wing. She looked down at it, then to me, and then went on with her story. "And then I see this, like, trickle of red light coming down from the ceiling, all around the outside of the lift's doors. That's weird, right?"

"What floor?" Marcus asked.

"The twelfth, my floor... and I saw this from across the hall and so I start walking towards it, to see what it is, see if maybe someone else was stuck in this dreadful place."

"You didn't notice that the halls were dark?" I asked.

"...I guess I did, that's why I could see the light so well, but I didn't really think about it at the time. I had just woken up, it was colder than a penguin's prick, and I was a little hungover from the night before, excuse me..."

"Of all the half-soaked things..." I trailed off, took out my own smokes. Her story was getting thinner and thinner. Maybe the kid's weed was just getting me paranoid. But I looked at Marcus and he didn't seem too impressed with her tale either.

"Then the door opens..." She pressed on with it anyhow. "And it's... Frankie. And my first thought was, 'oh fuck me, that's Frankie Gideon, he's fabulous.' I start walking closer and

I even shout something in case he doesn't see me but then I notice two things: The first is that Frankie doesn't look well. At first I thought maybe this is just what he looks like without makeup but then I could see it was something else. His skin looked almost green and he had this expression... The second thing was that he wasn't alone. Standing behind him was this... person. With his hand on Frankie's left shoulder."

"You didn't recognize him?" Marcus asked.

"I couldn't see his face."

"Was it all blurry and indistinct?" the kid offered. "A lot of ghost sightings are like that."

"No, and it wasn't a fucking ghost. The man, this figure... I couldn't see his face because he was too tall. He was so tall that from the outside of the elevator I could only see up to the bottom of the breast of his suit jacket. And that was at least a yard above the top of Frankie's head."

"That can't be right," I said. "How could this giant bloke even fit in the lift then? If he was that tall he would have to hunch in order to not stick his head out the roof of it."

"He stood perfectly upright from what I saw, and he wasn't just tall, he was wide too. Dark suit, his fingers looked pale, gigantic on Frankie's wee shoulder. He made Frankie look like a doll or a child in comparison."

"Did he look scared? Did Frankie say anything to you?" Marcus leaned in close to her, probably trying to figure out if she was telling the truth.

"I don't know how to say this without sounding terribly overdramatic, but I got closer to the lift and when I looked at Frankie's eyes he looked like somebody that was past fear. He looked like someone who knew he was going to die and there was nothing to be done about it."

"How do you know what that looks like?" the kid asked.

"Never you mind how I know but I know. I've seen it before." She didn't even sound angry at the lad for asking, more like she was tired of having to explain it and things like it. I knew the look she was talking about. I saw it in my mother's face when the cancer took her slowly when I was a boy. Saw the look reflected in my father's eyes as he watched her leaving. I believed Rikki, at least that part of her story. You don't have to be old to know death. "When I saw that look I stopped walking toward them. And then I saw that Frankie could see me, and then I swear I saw that big hand, that impossibly big hand, press down slightly on his shoulder, it was quick but I know I saw that, and then Frankie opened his mouth and this sound comes out. It wasn't a person's voice at all. It was loud, so fucking loud I had to put my hands over my ears. So I got away, started walking backwards down the hall. I was afraid to turn around and run just then. I didn't want to take my eyes off them. Then the noise stopped and Frankie shut his mouth and he grinned. And then the doors slammed shut and the red light came back around the lift."

"You said before that Frankie was going down," I said.

"I took the stairs down to the next floor but when I got there I hear the little ding and see that the bloody lift is there. It opens up and there's Frankie grinning with that massive hand on his shoulder and he's looking at me. So I take the stairs and make it down to the next floor, and I hear ding and there he is again."

"How many times did this go on for?" I asked.

"Enough that I stopped trying different floors and just went down the stairs straight to the lobby."

"And then you started running and that's when you found us?" the kid asked.

She nodded.

I had no idea what to make of this. Luckily Marcus did. His head tilted to the side, slightly at first. He looked at me, then the kid, and then Rikki. Finally he flashed his teeth and let out a belly laugh. "That's funny." He pointed at her face. "That is something else all right."

She didn't much care for it. "Well, I'm glad you think so because it wasn't fucking funny while it was happening, I can tell you that."

"It never happened." Marcus stopped laughing immediately. "I don't really care what any of you do here, whether you believe her foolishness or not, but I need to find my client and make sure I still have a job, so if you don't mind I'll be moving on now." He started walking past her and going towards the hall me and the kid came from that led out of the kitchen.

"I'm not lying," she said.

"Oh, I believe that you don't think that you're lying," Marcus turned back to say.

"And what's that mean?"

"He means you're probably high, love," I told her.

"You'd be the expert on that now wouldn't you, Mister Frivolous Black-out."

"Surely, you can do better than that," I told her.

"You're a lyricist for Christ's sake."

"It's no big thing, hell, I'm a little high right now too," Marcus said. "Finished a roach before I set to start searching for Frankie's ass. I'm not sure what you're on but we've all been there, seen some shit. Sometimes your substances can get the better of you. It's the peril of your profession. Back when I was working for The Doors I had to talk Jimbo down off a ledge more than once. And that's not a metaphor either. Fucking lizard boy decided he was Mister Mojo highrisin' every now and again; and no, he wasn't trying to kill himself, he just was

sick of his old lady giving him grief for getting his rocks off
with whatever women he had tucked away in his various Hollywood bungalows."

The kid nodded. "You can't let your anus give your grief."

"What?"

"Sorry, ah-nus."

Marcus tilted his head and gave the kid a hard stare. "...Yeah,
you better be honest."

I made no attempt to clear up any of this confusion, it was
far too lovely to trifle with.

"How did Morrison get his hair to do the lion's mane thing?"
The kid was a fountain that could not stop giving.

"I was not and am not fucking high right now," Rikki told
him. "I may have had a bump, like, last night but I'm totally
lucid right now, thank you very much. And yes, I know what
I saw makes very little sense and there may be some rational
explanation for it, but that explanation is not that I was hallucinating."

"What do you think, Codger?" the kid asked.

I wanted to tell him that I never in particular cared for The
Doors. That it was organ music, cabaret singing. I liked the
blues shit, you know? But my head shifted again and now I
didn't feel sick anymore, just out of it. Tired and impossibly
worn down like I could sleep for a day. Everyone's voice seemed
distant all of a sudden. It felt like when I was a boy and I'd
have my head in the grass and I could hear the other children's
voices and their steps muffled through the ground. It felt like
their voices were coming up from the dirt. The tiny voices of
children calling out to me from deep beneath the earth.

"Son," Marcus started. "Just comb your hair before you
shower, wrap it up tight in a towel when you're done, and then
let it fall as it will, you'll be breaking on through in no time.

Everyone else, this has been fun but now I gotta find my meal ticket and figure out how long we're gonna have to sit and wait 'til they clear the roads out there." He gave me a strange look that could be a cousin to pity and I figured I must have looked half as out of it as I felt. But then we heard the ding of the lift and he stopped moving. Impossible, the power was out. But the sound was coming from around the corner where Marcus had come from. Rikki shot me a look. "Well, guess that's Frankie and his giant monster then, right?" Marcus said.

He started walking around the corner and Rikki followed him. "Seriously," she told him. "I'm not joking here, man." I followed them both around the corner, naturally the kid followed behind me. We got there and the red light was still glowing, just like in Rikki's story, but the doors hadn't opened yet. There was another ding and then the doors parted. I saw Frankie Gideon, beautiful and strange Frankie Gideon. Thin as a nail, dressed in some silver and white jumpsuit with an enormous collar that stuck up, like if Count Dracula just had his balls removed and they were afraid he might get at his stitches. His hair was dyed redder than Mars, I almost thought it was a crown of blood resting there. The man was remarkable looking; he surely would have been a star even if he wasn't a brilliant songwriter and singer. But he was of course. He was also alone. No impossible giant behind him. But there was something off with Frankie, more off than usual: His skin didn't look discolored like Rikki said it was, it was his usual cemetery suntan, but there seemed an odd symmetry to him. Which was a weird thing to notice, but notice it I did. It occurred to me that the symmetry looked odd because it was. No one's face is really all that symmetrical. They say beauty is symmetry but it's just the approximation of it. True symmetry passes beyond beauty and what lies beyond beauty becomes terrifying. Unnatural. Frankie's newly perfectly matched face became scarred with the thinnest of grins. And then I saw it:

There was no symmetry, there were in actuality two different faces, inversions of one another that, like reflections in a funhouse mirror, collapsed back into each other at the center. These impossible half faces hovered over one another at the center almost perfectly creating the illusion of unity, of being a singular surface, but with movement, even the slight movement of a thin grin, their camouflage fell away and the horror of what they were became obvious. The faces crawled away from each other, coiling out of space like ram's horns sprouting from the air, revealing the halves to be in fact full and independent faces. And they were not alone. Somehow occupying this shared space, too, was a chain of more faces following behind the left and right leaders who had carved their spiraled paths.

Some of the faces looked like Frankie but others didn't even look wholly human. From out these dual cornucopia a sickly, weak green light emitted at the source. Even more dazzling was the light and color that seemed to drip off the collection of faces themselves in bright purple and yellow drops. They flickered and fell off into the air like shimmering fish scales or dancing embers. In the midst of all this I noticed a shared expression on some of the faces; more than one of them was smiling at me with a smug, vicious satisfaction.

"Holy mother of fuck," Rikki whispered, the first thing any of us had said since Frankie's presentation. Time felt strange then. I didn't know how many seconds passed between the lift opening up and then Frankie doing the same, but I know that it was only a brief moment later when I saw his shoulders hunch up and pull in. It was a fluid motion and it resulted in Frankie's space-vampire jumpsuit falling to his knees. His shoulders continued to move inward and up in ways that no human being outside a contortionist could pull off. Then they exceeded that and they no longer resembled arms. Frankie turned around, saving us any longer looks at the horror in between his legs, a first for him, of that I'm sure. And before I had time to question why the very forthcoming Frankie had suddenly become so modest I saw what he wanted us to look at. His back was riddled with small orifices like fresh incisions and from these openings light shone. The flesh making up the blanket of skin around them had changed as well, turning his back into some sort of glass honeycomb, like a sea sponge with a brilliant wet light coursing through its pocks and pinholes. A screaming meteor that was only fluent in pissed off rainbow. Now every one of the fresh horrible holes spangling his back blinked in unison and we realized that they were eyes. Eyes that spit dripping colors I'd never seen before. If I had not heard the sound his bones breaking made as the eyes blinked and cried color, I might have wept from the beauty of it.

Luckily, Marcus had a much saner response. "Hop to, let's get moving, people." He grabbed me by the shoulder and started to pull. But I couldn't turn away, not yet. I looked into the nebula of what had been Frankie's eyes, the space his face once occupied before it split. A shaky sort of apparition hovered there; it looked like human eyes flickering in and out, existing, then not, literally in the blink of an eye. And I could see behind these eyes, hanging in space, were even more eyes doing the same dance, twinkling like stars. They seemed to reach impossibly back like a row of dominos into the space where his head should have been. All of them studying me with listless intent; I couldn't tell if they were lifeless or so vastly intelligent it was impossible for a life form like me to register. I could feel Marcus pulling my shoulder, feel his spit on my neck as he screamed into my ear something about looking away, not getting hypnotized. Some sensible dreck like that which I was a bit too preoccupied to listen to at the moment. This was, after all, the glam rock changeling Gideon's greatest ever rebirth and I was front row to witness the neon afterbirth being expunged. Marcus' voice all but disappeared, as did the hotel, the snow storm, and the world that hosted them. It was only that chain of strange eyes and me. Nothing else. Then something happened. A warmth like midmorning sunshine hit my face and I only slightly registered that something had crawled into my eyes. A bit of that dripping color from the crevices on Frankie's back.

"Snap the fuck out of it," Rikki screamed at me. The warmth on my face had given way to a full burn. It felt flush, like it had been struck. Then Rikki slapped me again and confirmed my suspicions. I backed away from the lift, unsure how much time I'd lost staring into those strange eyes and their colors. But now I was back in control. "Codger, let's be on our way."

Behind Rikki and me, Frankie started slummocking his way out of the lift. His eyes caught mine and it took considerable self control on my part to look away and focus instead on Rikki. Admittedly she aided this endeavor merely by being herself. "Come on, you old twat." I did as instructed.

Despite her accurate assessment of me as an old twat, I found I still had plenty of life left in my legs and I charged down the hallway away from whatever the hell Frankie had become. Marcus had a flashlight and Rikki and I kept pace with him but surprisingly the kid kept lagging behind. He kept looking back over his shoulder, waving his own flashlight at the thing that followed us. I looked back at the kid to see how far behind he had gotten and caught a glimpse of Frankie through the flashlight beam. What little I could see didn't make any goddamn sense. I could hear him, or it, behind us, a sound like the humming of a dying electrical light, accompanied by a swish like a street sweeper. The kid kept on looking back; he was going too damn slow. "Lopez," I told him. "Josh Lopez, turn 'round and run." He didn't even correct me when I called him Josh instead of John. He was too far gone. But finally after a moment he turned his head and caught my eye. Something clicked and he started moving again. Passing me, and then up past Rikki and Marcus too. *You're welcome, kid.*

"In here." The kid flung open the door to the kitchen and we poured in. I got in last and turned around to help Marcus, who was waiting to slam the door shut. The door was thick metal and shut with a loud sort of clang. My face was next to Marcus' and we shared a look of relief. Then I felt a tremendous burst of pressure hit the door which made it sound like an aluminum can giving birth to triplets. The door swung back, throwing Marcus and me to the floor. I heard that electrical hum again and looked up to see a mass of long crooked fingers curling around the corner of the doorway.

Suffer a Witch

What was left of the faces that could still pass for human swayed in the air in two intricate, intertwining ribbons like a perfectly peeled apple skin floating in double helix before the last flick of the knife cuts it clean away. Lovely little thoughts like these filled my thick stupid skull as the screaming mess of what was Frankie Gideon charged awkwardly toward me on spindly stalks with a gait somewhere between a toddler and a tarantula. Like usual, everyone else had a more practical response to this.

Marcus and the kid backed up against the stovetops along a wall and Rikki disappeared behind me. I knew this because she called out for me to follow her, or at least get out of the way of Frankie. Sound advice. I couldn't look away but I did find my hand acting under its own, much more competent, volition as it felt along on a nearby prep table until it found a wooden knife block. The fractured human smile still on the ribbons of some of Frankie's faces curled up in a grin as he loomed over me. He also stopped making that terrible sound, and for a moment I felt my right mind creep back in. I could feel his fingers, his tendrils enveloping me. They did not feel unpleasant curling around my shoulders. They felt delicate and brittle, like corn husks after harvest. They pulled me in and I thought of the bleeding colors, what they had wanted to show me...

My butcher's knife found purchase right between the ribbons of Frankie's old face and straight into whatever bony, coiled structure was now boiling up from out of his neck stump. Apparently it was a face of some kind because it opened a mouth, or something like one, and screamed out in pain as I cut into it. I pulled back the butcher knife and a hot mist of bright yellow fluid hit my face and hair. I sunk my knife in again. Distantly, some part of me wanted to embrace the bent crumpled thing in front of me, but an even greater part of me rejected it. Wanted it dead. Wanted me to live.

Even when one of its tails or stalks whipped me back onto the floor I remember feeling relieved. If I was about to die at least I wasn't going willingly to the slaughter. I would die on my feet even if I was currently out on my ass.

Fleshy sorts of braids had sprouted out of the thing's limbs and some of them were coiling over my wrists, ankles, and neck as I tried to get up off the floor. I managed to get one hand free and ripped off whatever was wrapping itself around my neck. Like I had suspected from its previous touch, it was fairly delicate despite its strength. But as I tore through the tendril around my other hand I could feel many more curling around my side and pulling me closer towards their master. They felt like paper but were strong as a man. Maybe I was going to die here after all. I looked up at the bony mouth, much like a beak, a granite octopus' maw, as it waited for me, tongue sloppy in anticipation. I wouldn't look away, I told myself. I wanted to know this thing, needed to understand it in my last moments before it devoured me. Its breath was fetid and hot up against my face and I felt its wet warm tongue lapping against my face as I screamed—

But then a syrupy screech cut through the room, and again I heard the thing shriek, but now I saw why: Rikki brought her own blade down on one of the creature's longer appendages as it swirled around on the floor. "Come on, man. Get up." How wonderful that kitchens have so many pointy things in them. Rikki was just behind me, clearly terrified but being a lot more useful than I was on the ground. She brought her blade down again on the thing and it shrieked some more, sending her across the room with a swipe from two of its new black shining arms.

"Codger, move your ass." Marcus came around with the kid in tow. They both were carrying what looked to be plastic bottles in each of their arms: cooking oil. I took my butcher's knife and cut into whatever was still wrapped around me until I got free as Marcus and the kid splashed oil on the beast. Marcus yelled, "Codger." And I moved away quickly until I got clear. Marcus struck a box of matches against the wall and threw it at Frankie. The sound the thing made when it went up was even worse than its previous howl. It struck me then that this was because it had more than one voice. How many I couldn't say, but it sounded like an entire choir was burning alive and they were all screaming at once. Beneath this I could hear something inside it bubble then burst, over and over, as fire started to cook it. The smell was thick, foul, instantly washing over the room. Rikki ran towards the far side of the kitchen, behind a large prep table, and I followed her. The thing was completely lit up now, a screaming, thrashing candle. It paced and circled, parts of it moved out of its back like they were trying to jettison themselves from their own body. Jumping ship as their craft sank beneath the flame. The kid was going to run for it but I locked eyes with him and held a hand up, telling him to wait 'til the coast was clear. The thing was still spinning close to him erratically. Marcus picked up on this quick and held the kid back, then once Frankie fell to the ground, led the kid forward away from the still-moving burning mass towards the door. Rikki didn't wait for me to give her the signal; she didn't need to, she ran across the floor. A burning crooked arm reached out for her foot and she dodged it, but then another tendril of some sort whipped around and caught her other leg. It brought her down to the ground hard, and she let out a scream. Some other appendage that ended in a sharp point like the tail off a vinegaroon rose up above her back and she struggled to get back up. I moved without thinking, faster than I thought myself possible. I took the pointed tail in my hand, careful to grip below the point, and it spasmed like an eel in my grip as I cut through it with my butcher knife. Three short hacks, then a fountain of yellow fluid. Rikki got up and we got the fuck out of the room and away from the immolated rock star who had recently sprouted a dozen new murderous appendages.

For a few brief seconds things became sane again. The cool air of the hallway hit my face, cooling the sweat on my forehead that I hadn't noticed had accumulated. Even the storm outside, its ugly old song, was comforting. Because it was real. It was normal. It was the way things were supposed to be. I was running through a hotel hallway, something I've done a few times before, crazy nights when we were young and when being on the road with the band was still fun and exactly where I wanted to be… But now I was running in fear.

Nothing was the way it was supposed to be. "Come on, they went this way," Rikki told me and I nodded my head. We ran some more and I could hear Marcus and the kid's footsteps up ahead. They were headed towards the lobby. I knew this not exactly from memory, it was just the way most hotels were laid out. They all had different skin but the skeleton's usually the same. Like people, there might be different sizes, variations on color and other cosmetics, different types of plumbing, but the basic layout's still the same. Head on top, toes on bottom, and so on. Of course, there have to be allowances for some deformity. Every once and a while you'll find a lift that goes nowhere or a kitchen on the wrong floor...

But the Hotel Alucinari was resoundingly average. Normal. Except, of course, for its guests. We made it to the lobby and I saw Marcus and the kid standing dead in their tracks at the lip of the hall. "Why aren't you going for the door? Come on, fuck the snow, let's get out of here." Before Marcus or the kid could answer me I heard that familiar *ding* of the lift.

Directly across the lobby the lift rested, wreathed in that red light like before. The door opened. I expected Rikki's tall man. Or maybe Satan itself. Instead, out walked a woman in a black frock. Her dark hair washed down the sides of her face and back of her neck like the thickest of treacle. Where her eyes should have been there was only a slight glint embedded in shadow.

"Holy shit, it's the chick off the cover of the first album," the kid said and turned back to me. It was. It really was. The witch. The one who adorned the cover art of our eponymous debut record. It was a simple, beautiful, bucolic and somehow sinister and psychedelic image. Just a woman in black standing before an old mill surrounded by autumn trees wreathed in brilliantly red leaves. But the look on her face, it conveyed something otherworldly, haunting... It was one of the enduring myths of our group, that the band had never really figured out who the woman had actually been. Was she a model? Friend of the photographer of our first LP sleeve? What was his name again? Was she for real? A real bleeding witch in Birmingham? We never found out, so we used the mystery. Let it add to the lore. Besides, it was one less person for us to track down and pay. That was always something to strive for in this business. But here she was. And she looked exactly the same. Almost.

"There's something wrong with her," Rikki said. I didn't see it at first. Not sure if the kid did either. Not 'til it moved. But unwinding from the space behind her in the lift was something made of flesh. Something that was as dark as her eyes until it started slithering and winding around itself and then you could see its shimmer. When it moved it left brightly colored trails, something like the visual echoes you'd see after dropping acid. It was mesmerizing and oddly familiar. Maybe it was because it brought back that wholly stupid, in retrospect, but at the time profound revelation that every stoner stumbles upon at one point in their experience: What if I'm not hallucinating? What if I'm finally seeing things as they truly are? Rubbish. But the shimmering shadow trailed in Technicolor made a good point otherwise. Then when the witch's head lifted up and her mouth parted we discovered that the mass of shadowed muscle behind her was actually part of her. That it fed into her from behind, into her frock. Maybe into the back of her spine and behind her head. Using her like a puppet. A Punch and Judy show put on just for us. I heard Marcus whisper something fucking mad to himself. It sounded like... earworm? Then the witch's mouth parted even wider and out of it cobwebs of burning bright veins erupted into intricate and obscene new constellations that filled the lobby hall. An entire cityscape of blood-forged geometric snowflakes and it expanded towards us while she did the same. It was absolutely breathtaking. I took a step towards her. I wanted to know her. To understand her design that hung in its abattoir glory above me. And then the shimmering shadow behind her uncoiled some more so I could see its eyes. Which weren't eyes at all. Just two burning holes. And they saw me too. That's when it reached out to me.

The transmission, the signal, whatever it was, felt like someone forcing their dream through my skull. Trepanning its thoughts and visions in and relieving the pressure of my own consciousness. A pressure I never knew existed because it was how I experienced the world. But with it gone, with me gone, I was finally free. There was an emptiness there that was truly holy. What replaced or imbued me was a waterfall of roaring personality. I saw some bodiless, maybe boundless intelligence scattered in pieces along a dark sea of stars. Not sure if it was lost or hiding, only knowing that it roamed. It roamed but it was also everywhere all at the same time. Scattered and trapped. I saw a ferocious intelligence searching for form. And it searched for something more too.

I saw it walking on many worlds, all at the same time, in the same breath. Swimming through the murk of consciousness, blind from the flood of sights. But it wasn't deaf. The one thing it followed was sound. Music. Distant but audible, verging on discernible. I could hear it now too. I would say it was unlike any music I'd ever heard but that wouldn't be quite right. I had heard things which sounded like pale imitations before. A shoddily built simulacra of this exquisite sound. My music, for instance, the music of Frivolous Black... that was an imitation of this finer, higher sound. In this sound I could make out the distinct, hackle raising of the *diabolus in musica*, the devil's chord; the augmented fourth. I knew what this sound was. It was what we'd been chasing from our first song on once we started making doomy music. This was that sound. And this thing, it wanted it too. Needed it. I wanted to stay here, following the sound with this presence. To never return to the husk that was my body and mind, but something happened, a judgment passed, or a test failed, and the burden of my own awareness returned and I was cast out. And the pain in my head I'd been feeling since I woke up in my hotel room came flooding back.

"Fall back," Marcus said like he was back in Vietnam. "We need to get back to the kitchen." I came back to the world and everything was a screaming mess. The shimmering shadow behind the witch had turned away its burning eyes and was now advancing on us. The witch's weird puppeteer was still spinning the web from her mouth, but the shadow had separated from her and left her standing alone in the middle of the lobby. The others had already started to run so I turned tail and went after them. But just as I was leaving the lobby I caught something laying on the reception desk next to the cigarette machine where I first met the kid, something I could use. I watched the group disappear into the hall as I ran over and grabbed the axe as fast as I could. Behind me I could still hear the witch spinning her web. And I could still hear the shadow moving around, either chasing me or maybe just shifting around and getting comfortable. *Maybe it's just growing.* I didn't trust myself to turn around and give it a last look. Because I knew it'd be just that. So I kept moving and followed the others.

Hidden Forest

We made it back to the kitchen and slammed the door shut with no interruptions. We came back into a raining room. The heat must have set off the water sprinklers. "Smoke alarm is working, I thought you said the power was out?" Rikki snapped.

"It's not the smoke alarm," Marcus told her. "It's the sprinkler system and it doesn't run on electricity. Places like this already have water in the pipes, there's a bulb in there too, and if the room gets too hot it bursts and the water comes down." I didn't have to see Rikki rolling her eyes.

"It's actually not all water," the kid said. "Some of it is Halon from the fire suppression system, not the sprinklers; Halon is better for grease fires. See, water and oil—"

"Who asked you to fucking talk?" Rikki said.

"We need to barricade this door now," Marcus told us.

The water, the Halon, the wet shit from the pipes above, whatever it was, had already started to dissipate and I could see the charred still-smoking pile of what used to be Frankie Gideon lying there on the floor. The pile didn't stir, the blackened colony of limbs didn't twitch, the multitude of mouths didn't moan, and for all that I was thankful. Either it was dead or at least taking a good long snooze, so barricading ourselves in with it seemed like a bostin' idea. At least the thing in here might be dead; those two out in the lobby, the witch and the whatever, were definitely still alive. I looked at the kid. "We need to get some light in here, find candles or something." He went off and I put my axe down and walked over to one of the ovens. Then I pulled off a piece of the metal frame where some pans were being hung above and used it to bar the door with Marcus. Marcus ran over to one of the long metal prep tables and I followed him knowing what he had in mind. We almost ran into the kid who was carrying two plastic jugs in his arms. "I said light, kid, candles. I want fire, not water." He ignored me and then I returned the gesture and focused on the task at hand as Marcus and I dragged our prep table across the floor. It made a terrible racket before we put it in place in front of the door. I was about to go grab another piece to continue the build when a wash of white light swelled into the room. My first thought was that Frankie wasn't dead and he wanted to show us more of his wonderful dripping colors, but it wasn't Frankie, it was the kid. Next to him on one of the tables was one of the plastic jugs he had been carrying, only now it was glowing and producing a white light.

The kid was grinning. "Pretty cool, right? It's just a flashlight propped up against a water jug full of water. Learned that shit going camping."

"That's nice, son. Real nice," Marcus told him. "Here, take my flashlight and go make another one of those lanterns over on the other side of the room." The kid nodded, then started on it, and I felt a little regret that I hadn't been the one to give him the compliment. I wanted to be useful so when Rikki started trying to move another prep table I came over to help her. The second water jug lantern was set up and it gave the kitchen a dull glow like a TV set left on at night after everyone's gone to bed. "Is there any other way in here?" Marcus asked the kid.

"Just that door," he said.

"Wish we had a hammer, some nails," Marcus said.

"Do you think this will really keep it from getting in here?" Rikki asked.

"Don't know," I said.

"It might… for a while." Marcus held his hands on his hips, gave me a look like he was trying to convince me of it. We waited in the silence next to our barricade for maybe ten minutes. Without the rush of frantic activity, the necessity of survival jacking my heart rate up, I had time to finally register how fucking mad everything had just become. Frankie Gideon had reinvented himself for the last time and turned into some sort of light-spewing art rock chimera. In addition, outside in the lobby there were two creatures waiting for us: one resembled the witch off the cover of the first Frivolous Black album and the other looked like… well, like nothing I'd ever seen before. And yet, those burning dots for eyes…

The smell of charred glam rocker stained the air. It actually didn't smell as bad as I thought burning flesh was supposed to. I remembered talking to Marcus once about Vietnam and about burning bodies. He brought up the smell then. How it sunk into your lungs and weighed them down. How the blood in the victims' bodies gave off that burning copper smell. And underneath that, the flesh smelled like burning pork. Said it made him swear off barbeque when he got back to the states. Said it broke his mother's North Carolina heart but he couldn't eat that anymore. But Frankie didn't really smell like that, like a human being was supposed to. He still stunk, but it was different. His smell reminded me of something deep, dark, swampy…

Everyone had backed off to the far end of the kitchen near the freezers. No one was saying anything, just waiting for that

54   Tony McMillen

witch, or whatever it was that controlled her, to come crashing through our barricade. Quiet terror becomes boring quicker than you'd think. Thank Christ we had cigarettes.

"This is a kitchen then, knives, right?" Rikki said.

"Right," I said. We were kids in a candy store, only the candy was sharp shit that could kill someone. We armed ourselves with anything with a point, grabbed as many as we could hold. Having had some success with them already, I found myself two more good-sized butcher's knives as well as a smaller wok that looked like it could break faces. I decided then that butcher knives were the basses of culinary killing implements. I felt a kinship right away. Besides, Rikki had already helped herself to my axe. We also found some butane lighters, the kind used as crème brûlée torches. Those could be useful. Then we waited. Staring at the door, expecting something unimaginable to come bursting through any minute. "What does… it, they, want? Do they just want to eat us?" I asked the room.

"I don't think it's that simple," Rikki said.

"What is it then?"

"To make us like Frankie, to take us over?"

"If that ever was Frankie."

"What do you mean?"

"How do we know Frankie wasn't always like that? How do we know he was ever, you know… normal?"

"What, so he was always…" She put her hand up in front of her mouth and made like it was a spider on a treadmill.

"Well, it would go a great distance in explaining a few things about that weird fucking fucker, wouldn't it?" I said. It looked like she almost smiled from that. Humor's funny like that. Some of the best laughs I ever got were at funerals. Not cause it's terribly funny, the joke or the situation. It's just unexpected. Everything's funnier when you're not supposed to laugh.

My dad taught me that when we buried my mom.

"I knew the man," Marcus said. "I spent more time with him than I ever spent with my brother growing up. If he had been a monster I would have known it."

"Poor Frankie," I said.

"He was the master shapeshifter of rock, and now..." Rikki said.

I nodded. "I suppose he lived the way he died."

"What?" Marcus gave me a look.

"Oh, what I meant is actually... wait, *he lived the way he died,* is that actually accidentally profound?"

"No," Rikki answered immediately. "It isn't." I remained somewhat unconvinced.

"So Frankie was turned into that thing, he was infected, and now one of those three things want to turn us too." Rikki snuffed out her cigarette on the floor.

"Right, three..." I said. "The witch from the album cover, the thing behind it, and the tall man in the lift you saw." Even though her story about Frankie and the lift checked out I still didn't trust her. Her, Marcus or the kid. Each of their reasons for being here seemed a little flimsy. Right now the only other person in the room I trusted one hundred percent was Frankie because Frankie was dead. But regardless of her alibi for being stuck in this hotel, Rikki raised an interesting point: What if these things did want to turn us? Change us like they did Frankie? What if one of the people here in this room with me had already been changed? There was no guarantee despite what Marcus said that Frankie was ever human. Half of his bleeding concept records are about him being an alien from Venus or some shit; maybe that's what he actually was. Maybe Marcus was in cahoots with him. Maybe Frankie had already gotten to him a long time ago.

"I think they want you." The kid was staring right at me, pointing his finger nearly in my chest. In his other hand, a long cutlery knife.

"Come again?"

"They've come to collect, right? Like, on your soul. Like Robert Johnson and the fucking crossroads and all that old shit."

Not this shit. Not now. "Kid, are you fucking serious?" I told him. Marcus and Rikki had turned now and given the two of us their attention. "Let me spell it out for you… Heavy metal is bullshit. There is no devil, there are no crossroads, no pact was signed. I play scary music for pimple-faced high school dropouts like you because it's easy and it sells… least it used to." I gave Rikki an eye.

The kid stepped back. "I'm not saying we hand you over to it. I'm just saying you can level with us and tell us that you know what this thing is already."

"How much of that shit weed did you smoke before you found me in the lobby?"

"Tell them about the encounter that inspired the song 'Frivolous Black.' You were visited by this entity a long time ago. It gave you your talent and now it wants its payment for it."

"Wait," Marcus said. "Your band Frivolous Black has a song called 'Frivolous Black' too?"

"Guess what the name of the album was," Rikki said.

"The album too?" Marcus shook his head. "Sorry, Codger, that's just lazy writing."

"How is this news to you? It was our first song on our first fucking record."

"Look, I work in rock and roll, doesn't mean I listen to all of it. All that heavy shit is just noise to me. I'd rather listen to the Doobies or Stevie or Sly. Even Cream was all right. You guys are just too… sludgy." I nodded my head and smoked my cigarette. Man wasn't wrong.

"Come on, dude. 'Frivolous Black,'" the kid said. "Track one, debut album, *'Black form hovering above my bed. Black shape swirling into my head. I mustn't but it does insist, come forth, the black here is frivolous.'*"

"Please don't recite my early work back to me," I told him. "It's incredibly hurtful." Rikki actually did smile at that. "They're just lyrics, man. The band and the song are called Frivolous Black. *Frivolous*, we're taking a piss. Why do you Americans have to take everything so seriously?" The ache in my brain dulled as I raised my voice. "Little fucking conspiracy creeps like you are the ones who end up killing people like John Lennon. Little American shits who can't separate their fantasy from their day to day. Nothing happened, there was no encounter. No black shape with *'burning eyes like bleeding skies'* or any of that shite. They're just words that rhymed and fit a melody that Sully was singing."

The kid's face looked like it was about to break apart. Not break apart like Frankie, break apart in the regular way. He seemed to become aware of how he looked and put his knife on a prep table to our left. He dropped his hands to his sides. "I was just thinking that if the song was true maybe you'd know how we could stop it." Jesus, he really was sixteen.

"...I'm sorry, kid. I'm just a drug addict who can play the bass. I don't know how to stop from pissing myself most nights." I looked away but could feel the kid looking at me. I didn't like it.

Marcus stepped between us. I noticed him casually placing his hand on the prep table next to the kid's cutlery knife. Military training, or just being around enough stupid motherfuckers with knives in the vicinity to know when to be cautious. He looked over at me. "What the kid—"

"John."

"What John here is saying is pretty far out, but then again we're in a pretty far out situation, so…"

"So?" I said.

"So, is there anything to this? You ever seen any shit then like you've seen now?"

Yanks. Half-soaked, every single one. "I don't know… have you?"

"Come again?"

"Mister U.S. Air Force, mister Frankie's bodyguard, what have you seen before that you're not telling us?"

"So he was in the military, big hairy deal," Rikki said. "What, you think these are space men or something?"

"I don't know, Marcus, are they? What's 'earworm'?" I said it and Marcus' face dropped.

Rikki shook her head. "You really buy into all that cosmic shite you put into those songs of yours, don't you?"

"Of course he does, Frivolous Black is the truth, lady," the kid joined in.

I looked at the kid. "No, it's not." I turned to Rikki. "And I'm not saying anything, I'm asking stars and stripes here."

Marcus smiled tight-lipped. "You want me to be square with you?"

"Yeah, I figure we all might be dead any moment now so we might as well try and go out with a little honesty."

He laughed, that stage laugh of his. "Then how about you start. The kid was asking you about your song, 'Frivolous Black,' first track on an album of the same name by a band who either had a real shortage of ideas or really had a hard-on for those two words. You say the song's bullshit, some phantom encounter, deal with the devil, hoodoo shit that never happened. Then we see the witchy ass broad off the LP sleeve down in the lobby, only now she's got some sort of nightmare growing out the back of her. So, you want to be honest in what might be our final moments? Please, by all means, proceed."

I looked across the kitchen at the wet charred bones that used to be Frankie Gideon. "So Jim Morrison dies mysteriously in Paris back in '71 and now you set your latest client on fire. I'm starting to suspect you're actually a shit bodyguard after all." I did my own stage laugh. "Just how many rock stars are you planning to let die on your watch?"

"Always thought three was a nice round number. Besides, there's precedent." Jimi, Janis, and his old pal, Jim.

"If this is the kind of bodyguard you are, I hate to see how you fared as a soldier. How many of your boys never made it back with you?" I knew from the start of the sentence that I had gone too far. Marcus' eyes had bulged. He wasn't even trying to conceal the rage, almost waved it to me as a warning, *do not proceed.* But I did.

"What would you know about combat, about fighting in a war, especially 'Nam, Englishman?" He got so close our noses touched. "If this was any other situation other than our current I'd have made myself a nice pair of warm wet red gloves explaining to you exactly why you shouldn't talk about things you know nothing about, especially the men I fought with who did not make it back here to the world..." He took in a deep breath and it took every bit of nerve I had in order for me not to break his stare. "But here we are, in that situation, so I'm gonna just tell you, don't let me hear you mention my men again." I realized I wasn't breathing. Marcus leaned back on the prep table, out of my personal space, but his hand was practically wrapped around that cutlery knife and I exhaled.

"Codger, is there anything to any of this?" Rikki said. "I don't think I'm quite ready to swallow aliens from outer space but I have seen a bit of shit, haven't I? And it is strange that it took the form of the woman off the cover of the album."

"Are you secretly my biggest fan, Miss Spectre?"

She lit two smokes, walked over and wedged herself between Marcus and me, then handed me one of them. "I thought 'Suffer a Witch' was the single best song ever written except for 'Cosmic Dancer' by Bolan." I grinned like an illustrated definition of the word idiot. She smiled back. "Then I turned thirteen and realized what a sexist wanker song it actually was."

"Sexist? The song goes, 'I'd *gladly* suffer a witch.' It's all on the up and up."

"...Right. And the next line is 'if she'll lend me her stitch.'" ...So she had a small point.

"Fuck her, that song rocks," the kid said.

"Fuck yourself, you little ruddy cunt."

"...Old lady."

I think I actually snorted.

"What the hell does that mean? I'm not even thirty."

"Come on, man. Stop stalling," Marcus said. "All those years ago did you see something or not?"

I could still see those eyes. It was 1969 and I was living in a rinky-dink apartment in Birmingham, eating biscuits and thinking about a girl. There's a half-read copy of Aleister Crowley's *Book of Lies* face down beside me and I fell asleep after smoking a tiny joint full of worse shit than the kid gave me earlier. When I woke up I found I was still dreaming and I was no longer alone. I could still remember those embers floating above me then. Eyes of fire that weren't really eyes at all. Merely windows carved into some place that never stopped burning. Burning dots like I saw in that shimmering shadow in the lobby. But back in Birmingham I came out of it, woke up fully. And I was all alone again.

"It's all bullshit," is what I told them. "I had a scary dream, told Sully about it, and the next day Vinnie and I were listening to the 'Mars' part of Gustav Holst's 'The Planets Suite' and Vinnie got the bright idea to nick the tritone, the augmented fourth part of it. That's it, that's the story. I had a dream. Just a bad dream. And then I had a career." Of course I was lying. There was more to it. But even I didn't actually know how much more. Not yet at least.

Blossom of Corruption

"We need a plan," Marcus offered up.

"How about: *not get eaten*," Rikki said.

"They don't want to eat us, you said so yourself." Marcus walked away from us and the freezer and toward the open wet floor by the entrance. The water jug lanterns which showed his path were actually quite relaxing in defiance of the circumstance. But then I started worrying about how long the batteries on the flashlights would last us. We'd been in there under an hour, the things outside hadn't bothered us yet, but how long could that last? In fact, them not coming after us right away made me even more nervous. Because that might have meant there was no need to come get us, because one of us was already one of them. But that line of thinking only begged another question: If one of them was already in the room with us, what the hell were they waiting for? "Don't get me wrong," Marcus said. "I know what you mean. But how are we going to stay alive? How are we going to beat these things?"

"Apparently they're allergic to fire," I said and started walking behind him. I turned back to see if I was alone, but Rikki and the kid didn't budge. "So anyway, about this earworm business?"

Marcus didn't turn around when he said, "How about I show

you?" He picked up one of the flashlights and the water jug next to it and he walked over to where Frankie's scorched body lay. He put the flashlight back up against the jug on the floor, recreating the lantern effect. Only now the light was cast all over Frankie's remains. What was left there on the kitchen floor looked like an angel that had burned up upon reentry. All the new limbs, the stalks, fleshy and scaly looking branches and barbs that Frankie had grown, were now charred down and splayed out in wide wing-like arcs. Frankie's split-apart head, those two horns of plenty spilling out with trussed-to-gether faces, were now tattered and burnt into strange shards that looked like stretched caramel, not flesh. They stared up at us with a look of utter perverse delight. Each half grin, a meter apart, looked like some cracked Cheshire. If any of this bothered Marcus he didn't show it; he crouched down to look closer at his former paycheck.

"Jesus, Marcus," Rikki shouted from across the kitchen. "You really think it's wise to be getting so close to it?" My entire back had locked in tension and my headache seemed to bare down on me like an incoming train. Rikki had a perfectly reasonable reaction to watching Marcus do this. I was having it too. But she also seemed to miss the point of Marcus' behavior: If he was taking such an obvious and stupid risk, maybe it was because he knew what he was doing?

"I think he's done this before, am I right?" I said.

Marcus took his long chef's knife and gently dipped its edge into the right half of one of Frankie's more human-looking faces. It felt like time stopped. My hand gripped down on my butcher knife so tightly I thought the handle was going to break into my skin. I was expecting at any moment Frankie's light blue eye to spin back around and the teeth in his half grin to start rolling about their tracks like dancing piano hammers. But this never happened. Something only slightly less strange did. Instead of piercing Frankie's flesh, the tip of his blade seemed to slip into it without showing any sign of injury. The skin of his face coated the surface of the blade like a thick malt coats a striped straw. My hackle was still raised; faces don't usually coat the blades that push into them, usually they break and bleed, but no further activity happened and I breathed a bit easier. But even though the eye on this face of Frankie's was still a dull marble frozen in death, I peered down at it, knife gripped, waiting for it to blink. "To answer your question: No, I've never done this before. I've never had the opportunity to." Marcus pressed his knife in a little deeper and the blade penetrated and came out the other end, causing the skin to curl up over the blade almost to the hilt. He pulled the knife back and the flesh receded like the tide. "The last time I saw something like this we had the common sense to burn it then get the hell away."

"Vietnam?"

"No, I killed human beings in 'Nam."

"Fuck man, I didn't mean tha—"

"After my tour... I got home to the world and I started bodyguarding and I saw some things no one had many answers for. After... after Jim and what happened in Paris, Uncle Sam brought me in, told me they could kill me or I could help them keep an eye on other potential situations."

"So you were in Paris with Morrison."

"I went to check up on him."

"Mister secret fucking agent."

"No, just an errand boy again, only now I had a new errand."

"*Potential situations*' like Frankie?" Rikki had found her way to where we were. The kid followed close behind.

Marcus rested his knife on his knee and looked back at us.

"Yeah, like Frankie. Like Keith, like Janis, like all the rest I've guarded, kept an eye on."

"Did they know what you were doing?" Rikki asked.

"Shit, of course not. If I'd started blabbing about some unknown force that turns rock stars into monsters they'd have either fired me, laughed in my face, or made some unbearable concept album about it. Seriously, you don't tell a musician anything unless you want to hear about it on the radio in about a year."

"Wait, *Keith?* But he isn't dead," I said.

"Nothing can kill that man," Marcus said, then Marcus turned back to the body.

Instinctually I followed his cue. "Project Earworm was a project to monitor these... visitations. Different artists, musicians throughout recorded history have been approached by whatever this thing or things are. The U.S. Government only started really paying attention back in the '20s."

"The blues guys..." the kid said.

"Yeah, that's right. No one really put much stock in any of the stories, or if they did they didn't give a shit, not 'til some white hillbillies started dying too, in the '40s and '50s. Blues gave way to rock and roll and whatever this thing was followed it, or shaped it. We don't know."

"What does it want?" I asked.

"The only thing we can think is it wants music."

"What do you mean it wants music?" Rikki said.

"It seems to inspire or direct certain musicians throughout history who then in turn change the course of popular music." He said this with a perfectly straight face. "The early accounts are basically impossible to verify or separate from the usual weird shit that every fucking peasant or clergyman claiming to have been visited by angels or demons says they've seen; but if you look for it, it's there. Again and again, it's there. Steering things in one direction. Least that's how it looks. Later on in history you get all these great composers, Mozart, Beethoven, then Wagner, all these stories, myths of them being divinely or demonically inspired. Then the folk songs and the blues, then rock and roll, then…"

"Heavy metal?" the kid wondered.

"Punk rock," Rikki said with a certainty that I wanted to crush from her. Because I supposed it made sense. "But if it wants the music why the hell is it killing musicians?" she asked.

"Keith, Janis, Frankie…" I said it aloud not thinking I was going anywhere with the words. Then, "They're all washed up now or dead. They're done."

Marcus turned back again at me but didn't say anything.

"Wait, Frankie's last record was…" Rikki trailed off. "Fine, it was bollocks. His last three have been pretty hard to swallow if I'm being honest. And I love Gideon's work. It just seemed uninspired lately, right?"

"So," I said. "What, it gives rock stars their talent and then it takes it away and they either become monsters like Frankie here or just old and shitty like the Stones? Fuck… that's terrifying, I don't want to become like the Stones." Rikki shook her head in agreement. Marcus used his knife to poke at the beak-like growth that had erupted from inside Frankie's neck. It didn't have any unusual reaction, it was just dead bone or something like it. "What's the point of all this?" I asked.

"Point is, I've never had a chance to examine one of these things close up, and since we're stuck in here like pigs I figure now's as good a time as any to get to know our enemy. I learned what happens when you don't back in the jungle. My men learned it too."

"The hard way?" I asked.

"Better believe." He turned to Rikki who seemed to be looming over me as I knelt down. "I think I see something, you mind letting me use that axe real quick?"

"Sure, I'll just stand here with my thumbs on the ready to jam out someone's eye with."

I turned my butcher's knife around and offered her the handle. She hesitated, then took it and gave Marcus the axe. He flipped it around and took the blade to the middle of Frankie's exposed ribcage. He sunk the blade in like a crowbar underneath the bone and started to jimmy open Frankie's chest. It took a couple of good hard presses but then there was a wet crack and a smell like garbage left out in the rain hit our noses. Inside there was no heart, no lungs, none of the usual things you'd expect in any organism, even some glam rocker turned monster. What there were... were arms. Lots and lots of arms. They formed a sort of nautilus spiral, with the shoulder mounds growing from the center and the fingertips and hands lining the outside. Perfectly normal, human-looking arms. Growing out of the inside of this thing's ribcage for some goddamn reason.

"So you can explain this then?" I asked Marcus.

He shook his head. "No fucking idea, man." He took the axe handle and started moving one of the arms out of position. I wasn't sure why until he repositioned it so it no longer rested on the shoulder of the arm below it. On that arm there was a dark smudge and when I focused on it I saw that it was a tattoo. It read, *Herbert Malford II.* Marcus stopped leaning over and held his head up, shaking it slightly.

"Whose name is that?" I asked.

"That's his actual name," Marcus answered.

"I can see why he went by Frankie... Herbert. Stuffy isn't it? Rhymes with pervert..."

"He's a junior then?" Rikki asked.

"Yeah, he loved his father," Marcus told us. "I tell you, unlike our boy Frankie, the name Herbert fit a guy like his father well."

"…Pervert?"

"What? No, man. Just British as shit. Stuffy, rigid, wore a suit every day of his life until they buried him in one."

"Oh," I said.

"Codger, you idiot," Rikki said.

"I was just asking for clarification."

"Fucking Brummie," she said.

"Frankie loved his old man, looked up to him," Marcus said. "He told me after he started getting way out with the makeup and wearing dresses and shit, telling the press that he was into dudes as well as broads, that his father shut him out."

"Big surprise," Rikki said.

"Yeah. But it still cut Frankie. His father loomed large in his life, they never reconciled, and Frankie was out touring when the old man died."

"So he got the tattoo in tribute? Remind himself where he came from, make it right with the old man in some way?" I asked.

"No," Marcus said. "Frankie didn't have any tattoos."

"Yeah, he didn't," Rikki said. Marcus and I both looked at her. "Not that I studied him or anything, but I know, unless he got it since his last appearance on Whistle Test when he wore that brilliant green fishnet tank top and the eyepatch, he didn't have any tattoos on his arm."

"No, he didn't." Marcus laughed. This time it sounded authentic but it also didn't sound like it was because anything was particularly funny.

"What is it?" I asked.

"He didn't have any tattoos but he wanted one," he explained. "This one. This exact tattoo. Last year, after his pops died, we were in California touring. He had me take him down to a tattoo shop. Frankie was convinced he wanted this. I kept trying to talk him out of it. Told him it wasn't really his thing, doing anything permanent. He was more of a chameleon guy, you know? Besides, fuck his dad if he didn't like how Frankie did his thing. Last minute, before we were going to do the tattoo, Frankie disappears to the head. Ten, fifteen minutes pass, I go and check on him, he's passed out, and his blow is all over the ground and in the toilet."

"O.D.?" the kid asked.

"Shit, no. He was just exhausted. Frankie had been up two days straight, now he just had a moment of peace and quiet to himself in that bathroom. He probably felt himself crashing and he went to do something about it and ended up clocking out before he could get any more up into his nose. The guy at the shop was cool about it, told me to come back the next day when Frankie was feeling up to it. We left, next day Frankie didn't even mention it. He had moved on. It was just one of those things. He was a capricious kind of guy. Always getting really dead set on something then last minute totally not into it anymore."

I stared at the little tattoo on a perfectly human-looking arm resting in a circle of other perfectly human-looking arms that were growing out of a monster. "What are these things, aliens? Demons? Science experiment?"

Marcus turned away, rested on the handle of the axe like an old prospector after a long day of panning for gold. "It could be all of those things honestly. I mean, nothing's off the table. Fucking people's faces are splitting open and their backs are shooting out light. Shit, maybe it is the devil? Or something else that actually inspired man's concept of the devil."

"How can it... how can Frankie... how could Frankie walk around without any vital organs? A bunch of arms can't pump blood, you need a heart for that," I said.

"How about two or three of them?" Rikki had walked around the corpse and was near the barricade looking at it from a different angle. Marcus and I walked around with her and then I saw it. The light from the jug lantern bounced off the metal of a prep table and shined right into the top of the carcass. Sprouted like mushrooms on a log along two of the larger purple stalks that had grown out of Frankie's back were what appeared to be human hearts. Like the stalks they grew off of, they had been charred black and purple as beets by the fire, but it was clear what they were. Or at least what they were supposed to look like.

"Do you think it was trying to multiply itself?" I asked.

"Maybe," Marcus said. "But it was doing a piss poor job of recreating a working human being if that was the case."

"We were talking about a plan before you started on this dissection thing," the kid said. I looked over at him, apart from the group, keeping his distance from the thing.

Probably scared out of his mind, which I couldn't blame him for. I was feeling a bit more myself now, my headache was almost completely gone. I had that blessed second wind you get after surfacing from a day-long hangover, when you felt born again. Baptized and absolved from the sins previous and the night before. Still hungry as hell despite the charred monster at my feet. I was feeling better and I took a good look at the kid now with clearer eyes. Jesus, he was young. He kept his distance, looking like he didn't want his toes to get too close to Frankie's phalanges and other spread tendrils. But his face didn't look scared exactly. More nervous or exhausted. It looked like he was about to crack.

"Right now what we need to do is figure out a way to get past whatever it is out in the lobby—"

"The Earworm," I added.

"That was the name of the project, not the being itself," Marcus corrected.

"Well it's as good a name as any other for that thing that was behind the witch off of the album cover."

"Assuming we can get past it, then what next?" Rikki asked.

"We break through the door and get the hell out of this hotel," Marcus said.

"Doors are snowed in," the kid said.

Marcus shifted his weight on the axe handle. "Then we use some of them little fancy torches they use for those crème brûlées and we burn our way through it, son."

Rikki took out a smoke. "It's a blizzard outside, are you sure we can even burn through all the snow blocking the doors?"

"We could always get up to the second floor then try jumping out the window. If there's that much snow it should be able to cushion our fall, right?" I asked.

"'Jumping out the window,' fucking mad this one," Rikki said. "You wanna go first, have your legs snap, maybe if I land on top of you I'll only break an ankle."

"We'll use something, bedsheets, firehoses, something to rappel down," Marcus added.

"But what about the fucking monster out in the lobby? What about the other one, the tall man I saw in the elevator with Frankie? Did you forget about him? I sure as hell haven't."

The kid was staring down at Frankie's body. "…Why hasn't it tried to get in yet?"

"The thing in the lobby?" Marcus said.

"Yeah, I thought it was chasing us but it hasn't even tried the door yet."

"Maybe it's forgotten about us and gone outside now," Rikki said.

"Yeah, or maybe it doesn't have to get in here to get us." I stood up straight, took a step back from them.

"What do you mean?" the kid asked.

"Maybe it's waiting just outside the door for us to get stupid and confident then remove the barricade and peek our heads out so it can lop them off." I started walking away from them. "Or maybe… one of us isn't what they say they are."

Each one of them watched me, following me with their eyes as I moved even further away from them and Frankie. Towards the barricade and the door.

"You think one of us is like Frankie? Infected like him?" Rikki asked.

"Infected, I like that. I don't know, maybe you are." Unconsciously they all moved away from one another a bit.

"Whoa, now, we don't know that," Marcus said.

"We don't not know it, man," the kid said. This kid.

"Okay," Marcus said. "But if one of us was… like Frankie." Rikki put her hand to her mouth again and made like her fingers were snakes. "What's to stop them right now from… turning?"

My headache started coming back. "I don't know, maybe they saw what happened to Frankie and they decided not to make a move 'til they had reinforcements."

Marcus tilted his head slightly. "How do you mean?"

"Like maybe only one of us is infected, that'd be three against one, last time it was four against one. That's not much better then, is it?" I said.

"There you go, we were all fighting against that thing," Rikki said. "If one of us was another one of them why wouldn't it try and kill us then? Why would it kill the other one that was like it?"

"All I know," Marcus said, "is those things in the lobby are still probably out there. I don't know why they haven't tried to get in here yet but eventually they will and they'll probably make it in too. With or without our help."

"How long 'til somebody comes and finds us?" Rikki asked.

"Don't expect anybody to come," the kid told her.

"Why not?"

"Kid's right. The whole city's probably shut down, it might be days, even a week," Marcus answered for him.

"A week?" One of the jug lanterns started to dim ever so slightly. We all saw it. The light was dying.

Summoner of Sorrows

Sully Sullivan had never quit drinking. Hell, he had never really quit anything. Not even our band, even when he threatened to do it—which he did often enough—it was all idle. Sully never quit Frivolous Black because we quit him. Mainly because he wouldn't quit, the drinking, the coke and the chobbling up whatever pills people threw at him. None of it. Sure, he said he would, he cut it out for a few days or while we were recording but he never really quit. And right now, with the state I was in having quit myself, I could see why. It was coming back around on me it, it was, and I was having trouble hiding it. "Codger," Marcus said. "You don't look right." I'm sure I didn't. I felt unsteady on my feet all of a sudden.

"He does look a bit shit, doesn't he?" Doctor Spectre concurred.

I was leaned against one of the tables trying to wipe the hair from my sweat-soaked forehead and I noticed my hand had a slight shake. "I'm all right," I said in the strongest voice I could muster. "I mean, how am I supposed to look? Like a bleeding pop idol?" I felt cold everywhere except for my head; my head felt like a burn barrel being stirred with the devil's prick. The kid took a step back from me, running a hand over the table-top and working his way to a wood square stuffed with knives. When I saw the way he looked at me I felt like a leper looking for a handshake. "What do you want? For me to look like I did on your album sleeve, like I did ten years ago? Fucking kids…" Who was saying this? And why did the asshole have my voice? I was rambling, the room seemed to be swaying a bit as if we were at sea. Shit, I thought I had left the worst of withdrawals behind me back in my hotel room. But here I was, like any well-meaning yampy bastard, trying to plead my case and making it so much worse by the effort. I took a deep breath and tried to calm myself. "I'm all right. I am."

"How did you say Frankie Gideon's skin looked when you first saw him?" the kid asked Rikki. "You said it looked green, right? Did it look like that?"

And then I realized what they were really afraid of. "Look, I'm not going to… change like Gideon did." All three of them stared at me with varying degrees of apprehension. I tried to laugh. "Of all the half-soaked…" I stood up straight, raised my hands in gesture and then thought better and let them drop to my sides. "Okay, I get it. But I'm not turning into that." I pointed towards the glam barbeque off to the corner. "I'm just trying to give up the bottle. I've been sick as a dog for three days off and on, that's all."

"…he does look a bit green," Rikki said.

"Oh, you're going to trust her?" I shouted. "Where was she before she ran into us? She was the last person to see Frankie." I saw Marcus turn an eye to her. "And then afterward Frankie was different… infected."

"What the fuck are you on about?" She took a step toward me and the kid put his hand on a knife's handle.

"I'm saying of course you, the most likely of us to not be what she says she is, accuses me."

"I didn't accuse you, I said you looked like a fucking shamrock is all."

I watched the kid's hand on the knife. "You see how she's trying to get you to turn on me? You see that?" The anger was actually centering me a bit. Giving me focus, clearing my head. "I'm not some bleeding monster."

Rikki took another step forward, one hand pointed towards me and the other wrapped around the axe at her side. Behind her I heard the kid quickly pull out a knife from the block and then with a mind of its own my hand went for my blade.

"Stop. Everyone relax." Marcus got between me and the other two. "Put the knife back, son. Rikki, step back... please." They did what he said. "Codger, I believe you when you say you're trying to kick."

"...well, good 'cause that's all this is."

"I've seen it enough times to know what I'm looking at."

"All right." I let out a sigh and ran a hand through my hair then rubbed the back of my long-suffering skull. "Now can we focus on what's important. Dealing with th—"

"Not so fast." Marcus' eyes zeroed in on mine. "Look, I respect that you're trying to better your situation, I do, but unfortunately today is not going to be the day that your situation gets any better."

"What are you talking about?"

He looked back at the kid. "There's booze in this kitchen, right?"

"Yeah, I think."

"Find it."

"What is this? What are you doing?"

"Sorry, today's not the day that you kick, Codger."

I could feel my temper rising some more. "What the hell are you trying to do? Kid, don't do it. I don't want the drink."

"Do it," Marcus told him. The kid didn't move. "Look, you're in no shape to deal with what we have to contend with right now," Marcus said. "We don't need you shaky or weak, I'm sorry but we don't have time for that shit right now. We don't have any room for a liability."

"Liability?" I said. "Who helped you fend off that thing before? Me. Who cut at its tentacle thingie when it tripped up Rikki? Me."

"Yeah, but you also spent a lot of the time just staring at it in some sort of daze," Rikki said. "And I'm not trying to row with you—you are helping—half the time but the other half... you do seem a bit out of it and like you're going to get us killed."

I didn't like her being sensible. No, not one bit. "I'm dealing with extraordinary circumstances here," I said. "I'm allowed to be a bit zonked by it all, am I not?"

"Get something, beer, wine, liquor, just find something, son," Marcus told the kid. The kid for his part gave me a little remorseful look but then he turned and went off to the fridge. He had his orders, after all. Straight from his superior officer. "Codger, we're all dealing with extraordinary circumstances which means we need you at your best."

"Fucking tit-assed on hooch then? How is that me at my best?" The thought of a drink, of having to do this, all this, all over again was too much. My hands were still shaking only now it was plain rage. The kid came back into the room with two bottles, one looked to be gin, the other tequila. The kid brought four shot glasses. This fucking kid.

Marcus took the bottle of gin and two shot glasses. "We're not going to get you fucked up. We're just going to give you enough to get you back to functionality."

"It doesn't work like that. I..." I hated having them there looking at me right then, especially Rikki. But I said it anyways. "I have a drinking problem, you daft son of a bitch. The problem part being that I can't just stop. Not 'till I'm pissed."

Marcus opened the bottle. It was Beefeaters, my favorite gin. I could smell Christmas trees. "Codger, you know me, you know why they hire me: because I can out drink anyone. Morrison, Richards and Frankie too. I could out drink each of them and I could still get them to the stage when it was time for the gig. Which means I know how to pour and more importantly how to measure." He poured two shots, took one in his hand and slid the other one over to me on the table. "And right now it's show time, crowd's waiting."

"Oh, piss off with these extended rock and roll metaphors. I'm not drinking that shit anymore."

He threw back his own shot and tapped the glass on the table. He did so with control, it wasn't an angry, forceful slam but a measured almost dainty show of restraint. He looked at me, smiled and motioned with his head for me to knock back mine. I just stared at him. "Come on, it's not like you're drinking alone."

"Here, here." Rikki held the tequila bottle to her lips then raised the bottom up over her head.

"No," I told him.

He just smiled then poured himself another. "Okay, second round."

"I fucking quit, man. I don't need it, I'm fine now."

"Sorry, today is not the day you quit. Trust me, if we get through this I'll help you dry out. Hand of god, Codger, I'll be the first one waiting up with you at night if you go cold turkey or I'll be the first one to pick you outside rehab if you want to do this in style; but today is not the day. Now drink up." Again, I didn't pick up the drink. I folded my arms and stood back. Marcus gave a chuckle and then he knocked back his second drink. He punctuated this once more with a controlled but strong tap on the table. I could smell the liquor on the air.

The smell of gin always reminded me of my mother on weekends when I was little. Her breath when she kissed me before I went to bed. Something about it that I liked even though I knew it was a bad smell. Even when I had got a little bit older and she started to smell like it on the weekdays too while she was making us supper after she worked all day at the Lucas Auto Factory. Poor woman. Marcus poured himself another and I looked over at Rikki incredulous.

Her eyebrows were raised in seeming agreement. "Okay, maybe this isn't the best idea." She took another sip off her tequila. "One more for me... for courage and then I'm done. You want some, junior?" The kid took the bottle from her happily. She walked up right behind Marcus. "Right, so let's quit this now please."

"There's nothing to worry about it," Marcus told her. "I'm not going to mama bird his shot into his mouth for him or anything. But I think Codger wants a shot, just to settle himself. I think he'd feel better and I know we'd feel better if he did so."

"Actually I don't care anymore about that," Rikki said. "Now I think it's a bit fucked to make him take a drink when he's in the process of quitting. Know what I mean?"

"Thank you," I said. "Even the punker gets it."

"Weren't you getting close to certain that he was one of those things?" Marcus asked her.

"Well, no. No, I wasn't. He was accusing me and I was just observing that he was in fact a bit jade in his complexion. Besides he does look better now. And it's not like these things are allergic to alcohol, is it?"

"No." Marcus raised his glass. "But if Mr. Burton here would indulge me as well as his vices then if he started to appear healthy, maybe returned to his natural, pasty British complexion, then that might lead us to the conclusion that he was right all along and he wasn't infected as some of us feared. It'd tell us that he was just trying to better himself."

The look on Rikki's face didn't fill me with confidence. The kid took another swig and then made a face like a dog trying to get the peanut butter of the roof of his mouth. "I don't know, it does sort of make sense, Codger." Rikki shrugged.

"Unless Marcus is the one who's infected and he's trying to get us all pissed so he can get the jump on us," I said. Rikki and the kid weren't convinced.

"Besides, at the very least it'll solve my problem with him," Marcus said. "He has a drink or two and I won't have to worry about him being a vegetable when the enemy comes for us."

"Honestly, Codger," Rikki said. "He has a point, right?"

"Goddamn it, woman, pick a side!"

Marcus clinked my glass with his own and I swear the smell from the small bit which splashed and dribbled out from the glasses went straight up my nostrils and my heart grew three sizes. Marcus had that fuckface grin on his fizzog and I couldn't stand it. Fucking Yank, fucking army man Yank, puffing out his chest trying to push me about. *Won't have to worry about him being a vegetable when the enemy comes for us. The enemy,* he was still playing solider. Bossing about Rikki, the kid and now me. Then I had an idea. He was just about to speak again when I beat him to it. "You want someone to drink with so bad at least make it interesting for me. Go on, tell us about the war."

Marcus' glass lowered a bit. "Now I already told you not to bring up any of that."

"And I told you I didn't want anything to drink. So you want me to drink, I'll do it." I picked up my glass. "But I only drink when I'm depressed, so why don't you tell me one of your sad little stories about your friends getting their legs and arms blown off in that fucking jungle; tell me all about your friend Charlie running around in the bush cutting off their peckers and shoving them in their mouths. Tell me all about your men, the ones who didn't make it back, which, judging by your track record as a bodyguard, is probably all them. Please, do tell me all about it, I'm quite thirsty and could use the sniffle." I'd never seen such contained, razorblade hatred in a human being. Marcus' face was still as a churchyard but his eyes looked as if they could leave his skull at any moment in some mad plot to kamikaze into my own.

But instead he dropped one of his stage laughs. "You got some balls, Englishman. I'll give you that. But you keep on talking like that and you're bound to lose 'em." He took his shot. A grin cut across his face as he savored it. Then he let his glass hit the table hard. "So what do you want to know?"

I wasn't prepared for this. "Come again?"

"Get your glass ready. Ask me something specific and I'll give you your answer."

As he poured himself another round I mulled my options and supposed there was nothing left to do but call his bluff. "Did some of your men die in 'Nam?"

"Yes—I thought that clear by now—drink." His eyes locked onto mine. I took up my glass to my lips, hesitated then took the shot. Burning gold ran down my throat. God it tasted good. I put my glass down to find Marcus doing the same with his. He snatched my glass from my hands and then poured us both another round. "Come on, that was an easy one, what do you really want to know?"

He pushed my glass over to me, the bastard. So I asked, "How many? How many of your men died?"

Marcus had a smile on his face. "Ah, now we're getting somewhere." He lifted his shot glass, his eyes stared back at me from over the brim. "We had nine men in my squad, just the two of us made it back." He nodded his head as if in agreement with something no one else could see. "Okay, drink." And we did. And we both slammed our shot glasses down.

"All right, I think he's good, Marcus. I think you're both good," Rikki said.

"No. One more. And don't worry about me, this would be a Tuesday afternoon as far as me and Frankie were concerned. One more question, one more drink. I want him right. We need him right."

"Codger, you're better now, yes?" Rikki asked.

The slight burn of the gin felt damn fine going down the pipe. I was already feeling a bit more myself after the two shots. So maybe that's why I let the devil in me do the talking. "I'm still curious if he's still looking for a drinking partner?"

Marcus poured us our round and put the glass in my hand this time. My hand became a fist around the glass. "So these friends of yours, the ones who never made it back to the world with yo—"

"*Back to the world?* You're saying that like you know what that even means." He shook his head and snorted. "I use to think like you, you know that? When I first got to 'Nam, heard guys talk like that about getting back to the world. What they were going to do when they got back to the world. The things they had planned. The jobs waiting for them. The women. The family. The future."

"But they never made it back," I said.

"No. You don't get it. There ain't no going back to the world. Not for anyone. Not for me. Because once you leave the world behind, even if you get back to it, it's already moved on and now it's you who's left behind. It takes a while to figure out but soon enough it hits you. There ain't no going back." He went to knock back his shot but then stopped himself at the last second. "Oh excuse me, almost forgot, what's your question?"

I didn't want to play anymore but the look on his face told me not to upset the game. "...was it your fault that they died?"

He hesitated, something behind his eyes shifted. "Yes. Yes it was. I was their sergeant. And I made a very stupid mistake." He took the shot, slammed his glass down. "And those men, those boys, they died on account of it. Each and every one. Yes, they did." He looked back at the kid. The kid just put his head down and pretended to read the label on his tequila bottle. Marcus looked at me, then his eyes fell to my full glass. I knocked it back, welcoming the burn to my throat.

"Okay, that's the last one then," Rikki said and she reached for the bottle of gin.

Marcus slid it away from her slowly. "Last call, I'll give you one more, Codger. What do you want to know?"

Rikki looked to me like I had any idea what to do. So I said, "Sorry, I'm not feeling thirsty anymore."

And Marcus laughed. He poured two more shots. I backed away from the glass and Marcus laughed some more. "Ask me if I remember their names?"

"What?"

"You heard me, now ask."

"Fine, what were their names?" Rikki asked.

"No," Marcus snapped. "This is between me and the drunk. Ask me, Codger."

"Do you remember their names?" I asked him reluctantly.

"Yes I do. Garrett Cook." He took his shot, slamming his glass down and then pouring another. "Daniel Cleri." He raised his glass, seemed to wait for me to do the same and when I didn't he took the shot without me and filled his glass again. "Aaron McGrath." He took his shot. "David Keaton." He took his shot. "Nick Fimbers." He took his shot. "Chris Irvin." He took his shot. "Glenn...Glenn Lawrence. I never even liked Glenn." Marcus looked down at the shot, the corners of his mouth curled in a blissful grin. Then he brought his head up and looked at me and I saw the tears spilling from his eyes. And as they ran down his face I didn't know what to say. Because there was a moment when maybe I could have said something. Something to tell him that I saw him in pain, that I was sorry. That even if I could never understand what he'd been through that right now he wasn't alone. Anything. But it passed. Marcus had taken his shot. And then I took the only one that I had remaining.

Year Without A Summer

Marcus became tremendously drunk and pissed himself. In fact he was rendered so utterly useless from the ten (or was it eleven?) shots that he imbibed that we used his passed out, piss-soaked body as a decoy and pushed him out the door of the kitchen and made a run for it while the monsters came and ate up his body and probably became quite shithammered themselves from consuming such a pickled and combustible piece of meat. That is what absolutely should have happened. But no, Marcus was as his reputation stated, a drinker of such uncanny talent and unimaginable threshold that he didn't even appear to have as much as a buzz. Though admittedly it was hard to tell, seeing as no one in that room was saying a goddamn thing to each other anymore. Though on the brighter side thanks to being forced back on the medicine I was feeling positively bostin'. Well, not quite but my headache had left me.

I was used to waiting around in tense rooms thanks to being in Friv for all those years, so what came next felt natural. Four people who didn't really trust one another, sick to death of the dumb looks on each other's faces, but stuck together in order to survive. And at least one of them (me) was a dredged up addict who was no use to anyone. That used to be Sully's position in the cosmic scheme of things but now it was mine.

I was never much on Tarot, but I had a girl at one time who was and she used to give me my future. It always seemed to revolve around the "Fool" card. She'd tell me this was a good thing, the fool symbolized the beginnings of a great journey or some such nonsense. This was around the time we'd just released our last record with Sully, *Friv Today, Die Tomorrow*—no I'm not going to apologize for the album title—and I was in no mood to hear anything about the beginnings of something great. In my mind, starting with the last two records before *Friv Today*, each album we made was worse than the one that preceded it. Which made this new one the worst thing we'd ever made. We had reached an all-time low in communication with each other, especially Sully. He could barely keep the lyrics straight I'd give him when we recorded. On stage he was a fucking slob; he had always been a nutter, hell, that's why we hired him, that's why we loved him, but now it wasn't a good time. Now it wasn't fun. It was obvious he was in pain, that he was out of control, and like any other group of equally damaged young men we promptly turned our backs on him when he could no longer keep up. But before we did, even though it was already practically a fucking certainty that he was out of the band, we made that last god-awful album and tried to drag ourselves through one more tour to support it. To give the marriage one last shot. If the old cliché has any teeth and bands are like marriages and the stage is the bedroom and playing live is sex. Well, we used to always be good in the bedroom no matter what. But now things were humiliatingly bad. The chemistry was gone, no one was getting off anymore, and our then-private lack of connection and intimacy reenacted itself in front of thousands nightly. I suppose if the live show was our sex life, that made our albums and our songs our children, and the last few had all come out half-formed, stillborn, or just shrieking masses of too many limbs and not enough eyes. Monsters. All of them should have never been carried to term. I didn't blame them, of course, like all children it wasn't their fault, it was the parents'. But like many a failing marriage before us, Frivolous Black thought a couple more kids might save our relationship.

The new group I was in now, barricaded or trapped in that kitchen, was just as doomed. And I trusted them just as little. Sure, Marcus—who was keeping to himself at the edge of one of the tables after his one-man endurance contest—had confessed knowing something about this Earworm business. So what? He had told us about having a knowledge of these creatures and whatnot, but I still wasn't sure about his intentions. He had lied to Frankie and all the rest of his clients over all these years which meant he was practiced at it. What was his objective besides simply monitoring these visited musicians? What would he do to me if we survived this? Would he hand me over to some clandestine government agency? Would I end up in some underground bunker that'd make the Japanese Unit 731 and the Nazi medical experiments look like a holiday camp by comparison? I couldn't trust Marcus. Besides, he was a Yank. Then there was the kid. Another Yank—albeit a Mexican one… I think—who didn't appear as if he knew anything, even about this shitty hotel he worked in. The only thing he did seem to know any amount about was me and my music. Young people and trivial fucking knowledge. And he seemed pretty all right on giving me up to that thing out in the lobby, the Earworm. Maybe it was just the Lennon shooting still murking up my mind, or the shit weed the kid had me smoke earlier, or, you know, the layer cake looking monster that had become of Frankie Gideon, but I was well into getting serious paranoid vibes from this whole situation. The kid looked like he was going to fish-gut me with that knife of his earlier. Of course now he just looked down mostly, leaning against the freezer door, probably traumatized, the poor sod.

And there was Rikki. Spectre I trusted the most, or I suppose I distrusted the least. First off, she was British, which helped if I'm being honest. She was half Somali, father's side I think, but she was born and grew up in England and that made all the difference to me. Even if she was a London girl. One who called me fucking Brummie, I might add. Second off, she was sort of famous. Which I knew sounded really superficial and callow, but when you're sort of famous you learn it's hard to trust anyone who isn't famous too because everybody else wanted something from you. Your lover. Your friends you had before. Even your father. Everyone. At least most of the other lucky fuckers who get to be in *Hit Parader* or *Rolling Stone* aren't trying to wring some more money out of your neck. At least not usually. But still, even with Rikki, something seemed off about her. About her story. I couldn't put my finger on it quite yet but something didn't add up. "You never told me why you didn't evacuate with everyone else, Rikki."

She was leaning over a prep table, smoking and staring at her axe blade. "Yeah I did, sleeping. Nothing special, I was sleeping when they knocked on my door, that's all." She looked up from the blade. "You never told me what you were doing here that was so important that you missed the bus either." She sniffed her nose and ran a finger under it then gave me a look.

Smartass. What pissed me off the most was that she was right, I was a cokehead, and a drunk, but she was also probably not much better. She was just younger, putting shit up your nose and drinking 'til you blackout every night was still a total gas to her. For me it was just medicine, insulation from reality. I was old, my band had turned to shit, and now I was going to die with some punker who thought they were better than me. "Similar story, only I was asleep in the bleeding closet because I was all fucked up trying to kick booze and coke for the last few days. As I said before." I might as well have stuck my tongue out and pulled on my ears. Rikki didn't flinch.

"Fuck, I could use a little blow right now."

"What a tulip you are, dear."

"Fucking baby, I'm not your bleeding mother so don't expect me to coddle you, Codger." She delivered it without even a hint of anger. An even, toneless voice. Like getting admonished by a robot, you couldn't even enjoy that you had gotten a rise out of someone else.

I laughed. I wanted it to be mean at first but it wasn't. So I kept on laughing. And then she laughed. The kid smiled along. And then even Marcus from his corner of darkness chuckled. Funerals, everything's funny at a funeral. Best comedy club there is. You'll never get better laughs than at a funeral. And if anybody doesn't laugh, well, fuck 'em, the stiffs. "You remind me of my mom, actually. Way you're holding that axe and looking at me."

"Sounds like a sensible woman," she said. She took out her pack of smokes. I eyed that there were only two left in the pack, she popped one in her mouth then passed the pack over along with her lighter. Class act, that one. I showed her my own pack but gave her an appreciative smile. She lit up then asked, "Anyone else hungry, 'cause I'm fucking starving."

"They have some stuff in the fridge, I could totally get you whatever you want," the kid said. Little fucking idiot, god bless and keep him. I remember turning into a jelly every time a pretty girl ever talked to me too. It was kind of adorable and definitely sad. Like a puppy with one of those wheelie things attached where its hind legs used to be.

"Yeah? If you really don't mind, I'd eat anything that doesn't have meat in it."

"Uh…" The kid looked like someone had asked him to recite Pi.

"Not for nothing but this might be the last thing you ever eat," I said.

"What do you mean?"

"Well, if you're a vegetarian because you find the taste of meat repulsive that's one thing," I said. "But if you don't eat meat because of moral reasons, well, you might be dead very soon, so you might as well do whatever the hell you really want because you're not going to be around long after to feel guilty about any of it."

"Hmm," she said. "I applaud your dodgy reasoning skills." She turned towards the kid. "Okay, fuck it, I'd like a steak, no wait, you'd have to cook that wouldn't you…"

"The cold fried chicken is lovely here," I offered.

"Okay, one of those then please." The kid seemed relieved and opened the fridge door.

"I'll get in on that too if there's enough," Marcus told him.

"Codger?" the kid asked.

"Naw, I'm good for now, thanks… John." I just wanted him to know I actually did know his real name. Just so I could tell myself I wasn't such a prick. He disappeared into the fridge. I liked the kid. Even if I didn't trust him, I liked him.

Even though the bird was cold you could still smell the spices on it. It was heavenly. "Fucking Christ I'm excited, it's been years since I had anything that actually tasted good," Rikki said.

"You think the smell will attract the Earworm?" I asked Marcus.

"I don't know what will or won't attract that thing, except for you."

I thought I heard a slight slur in Marcus' voice. Then I said,

"Why me, I'm the bass player?"

"But you're the lyricist too," the kid said. "And you're a fucking great bass player. You're Codger Burton, dude. The 'Beast of Bass' the 'Lord of Low End.' On 'Tetrahex' alone you prove you are not to be fucked with. I'm not trying to kiss ass or nothing but you're easily almost as good as Entwistle or John Paul Jones and both of their bands can't hold a candle to Friv."

What could I do but take the compliment? "Thank you, I suppose. But I still don't think if Friv's music is anything special it's on account of me and my contributions. All our songs start with a riff from Vinnie, he's the real architect of our sound. We build off of that, everything we do is in support of the riff. Sully's melody, my bass playing, Burt's drums, and then my lyrics, they're all there to support that riff from Vinnie. Why isn't this thing after him?"

"Why heavy metal at all anyways?" Rikki said as she bit into a crunchy breast and started making obscene sounds as she set to chobbling the fried bits. "Ohsweemothroffuckgawthasgood."

"It seems to be moving the music towards a certain direction," Marcus said. "Blues, rock and roll, hard rock, psychedelic, heavy metal… it's shaping things towards harder and harder sounds. You know what I mean? Things keep getting progressively louder, harsher. It wants the artists who steer towards that aesthetic." So, he was that sort of drunk.

"I actually prefer mellower music," I told them. "If it was up to me we'd record an entire album like the songs 'Hidden Forest' or 'Year Without a Summer.'"

"Ugh." The kid sighed. "The acoustic songs?"

"That's some of their best work, twat." Rikki jumped to my defense. She looked as surprised as me after she said it. "If you go for any of that old doomy, heavy bollocks."

"Yeah, 'Year Without a Summer' was actually slated to be the title track off my solo album until I lost my balls and scrapped the entire idea."

"You were going to do a solo album? Were you going to sing?" Rikki asked.

"No, god no. I wouldn't subject anyone to that. It was going to be real arty, instrumentals, maybe some spoken word on the top. Trippy, mellow stuff, maybe even sitar on some tracks. I had even booked two weeks in a studio to see what I could accomplish but luckily Vinnie talked me out of it."

"Luckily?" Rikki said.

"Yeah, can you imagine what Frivolous fans would have thought?" I pointed at the kid. "They barely tolerated that type of shit on our proper records, imagine what they'd do when presented with a whole album of like-minded tunes?"

"I hate that... people's expectations." The smoke spilled up from her nose in a crooked arc. "I mean, sure, it's a nice problem to have, to have people who think enough of what you do to have an expectation at all... but then you get stuck, like you, afraid to do anything besides what you know and what they know you can already do. There's no way not to disappoint. I hate that."

"I'm not trying to be a dick or anything," the kid said. "It's just 'Hidden Forest' really drags down side one of *Schizoid*. Especially sandwiched right after the title track and 'Tetrahex' which are both so fucking rockin' and heavy."

"It's called diversity and dynamics," Rikki explained. "You wouldn't want every song to sound the same, would you?"

"No, I don't. All the heavy ones are heavy but they're still all different. It's just like... I don't go to Frivolous Black for chilled out jams, I want them to rock my fucking balls off, you know? And sound all evil and sinister... and shit." He added the last almost meekly. I had never heard "and shit" uttered this way before.

"I'm sure there's many who agree with you, kid," I said.

"I always thought the title of 'Year Without a Summer' was lovely." Rikki tore out a large portion of white meat like a cat playing with a dead mouse.

"Yeah, me too," I said. "The title of the song comes from 1816 when Mary Shelley and Lord Byron and the rest of that mess were stuck up in that house telling each scary stories, doing opium, and probably shagging each senseless while it rained all summer long."

"Wait, who's Mary Shelley?" the kid asked.

"What's this? Finally something the kid doesn't know about one of my songs."

"Mary Shelley, man," Marcus said, taking a bite out of a large wing. "You know, the broad that made *Frankenstein*."

"You mean Frankenstein's monster," the kid tried to correct him.

"No, I'm talking about the book *Frankenstein*. She made the book. It's perfectly fine to just say Frankenstein when you're talking about the title of the fucking book and not the monster itself." He shook his head and swallowed his bite. "People need to quit with this Frankenstein's monster semantics shit."

"Sorry," the kid said. "I didn't even know it was based on a book."

Marcus tilted his head. "Really? What do they teach you in school?"

"I'm graduated." The kid looked at Rikki.

"You're graduated? Don't tell me that, how old are you, son?"

"Look it doesn't matter, I was homeschooled so I finished early."

"Homeschooled." Marcus nodded. "There it is. I've been wondering what was wrong with you, my man, and now I got it."

I laughed. The kid wasn't sure how to react. "What do you

mean what's wrong with me?"

"No, no. Don't worry," I told him. "I think he's just taking the piss."

"What the fuck, dude? You're making fun of me?"

"More like having fun with you," Marcus told him. "But your reaction proves my point: homeschooled kids are weird birds."

Rikki was being strangely quiet on the topic so I gave her a stare. Finally she spoke, almost reluctantly, "I don't know... I mean I was homeschooled."

Marcus and I erupted in laughter. "Well, there you go."

Rikki sighed, shook her head and tried not to smile.

"What's the fucking deal? Why am I weird?" the kid asked.

"You're fine, son. You're fine. You all just haven't developed the social skills that everyone else has."

"What, because I don't know that Frankenstein was a book before it was a movie and a song?"

"No, because you're freaking the fuck out about it," Rikki said. "You'll be fine. I ended up just fine. And I think being homeschooled was rather quite nice for a lot of things. Though I did run away from home when I was thirteen."

"Why?"

"Why do you think? I was homeschooled and bored out of my goddamn mind. Any time I met another kid I had no idea how to interact. I either acted like I was a little adult who didn't know how to play or have fun at all or I was so inexperienced compared to the other kids that I was treated like I was retarded or a little sister who wanted to tag along." She laughed. "And on top of that I was Somali so automatically most of the kids I met were white and treated me like an exotic fish and stared at me when they thought I wasn't looking. I was always looking! How could I not look? Or they just fucking hated me outright. And on top of that my father raised me Muslim so there was another thing to make me different. And then there was some of the other Somali kids who treated me like a half-breed and didn't want a thing to do with me either." She looked at the kid. "Look, you're awkward because you're earnest. Earnest is just another way to say you say what you mean. Nothing wrong with that, in fact I think the whole world could use a bit more of that. All you're missing is the ability to bullshit, that's the ability that all the other kids pick up on and get good and practiced at in school. And you know, it is important, because this world runs on that bullshit. So you'll learn, like I did, eventually, to do it too. Even if just a little bit. But…" She flashed a smile at me and Marcus. "Don't ever feel less than for being real. Because the world may run on bullshit but it's honesty, cold, hard, fucked up honesty that is going to change it. So, don't lose all your awkward, mate."

Marcus had a profound look on his face. "Oh… Somali, you're half Somali? This whole time I was like, is this sister Egyptian? She got a little Indian in her? But Somali, that makes sense."

"Motherfucker." She threw a chicken bone at Marcus. And me and the kid laughed along. I took out a smoke, walked over and offered the pack to Rikki who shook her head and grabbed the last piece of chicken. I offered it to the kid next who took one with a grin. The smell of the chicken was getting to me. So I put my smoke back in my pack and walked toward the fridge, hoping to get myself either something savory or maybe even some ice cream if they had a freezer. "Hey, if you want something I can get it for you," the kid said while trying to look cool for Rikki with the cigarette in his mouth.

"No need, I'm fully capable of looking for myself." I opened the fridge door and the cold hit me. I started thinking about the storm outside, how cold it would feel if we ever got out. It wouldn't be that bad for long. We were in the heart of downtown Boston, even with the streets clear we'd find a place to stay. We'd smash windows if we had to. If the police came then great, we could tell them to get their monster gear and go back to the Alucinari Hotel. The door slammed behind me and then I was swallowed up by the dark. I took out my Zippo. Even with the power off the room was still cold enough I could see my breath. I crept in at a slow pace. Everything on the shelves was covered in plastic wrap or still in a cardboard box; maybe I should have had the kid fetch my food for me. But the thought of him bringing me my food bothered me. *Infection*, Rikki had called it. Whatever had happened to Frankie. What if there was truth to that? What if the kid was already infected and now passing off the bug in our food? What about before, the cigarette Rikki had given me from her pack? The one I took like a fool even though I had my own. Hers weren't even my brand. The paranoia was bottomless, it was making me lose my appetite. But at the back of the room I saw another door for the freezer. For some reason I've always fancied ice cream when it's cold outside, don't know why. So I went in there.

The room was terribly cold and I almost turned back but then I saw something that didn't belong. On the ground, sticking out from behind the right shelf, down near the condiment tubs—feet. Two feet and legs laying on the ground, sticking out from around the corner. I walked around the shelf and found a dead man covered in frost. He was brown-skinned with short hair, wearing only his underwear and an undershirt, on the floor with his eyes open. An ice patch of dark brown, a waterfall of frozen blood erupted out of his neck and down his belly. Next to him there was a pile of clothes. I crouched down and rifled through them; black jeans, a denim jacket, and a pack of smokes. Cherry Valleys too. Admittedly, I felt like a dirty fucking bastard when I pocketed them, I did, but seeing him dead like that was just further proof that this might be my last pack of smokes so I might as well take 'em. Besides, it was my brand. If there was a god in charge of this miserable series of events, this was one of the few bones he had thrown me as of late.

I looked at the corpse closely, trying to determine if he looked changed, the way Frankie had been changed. He looked human. Then again, I hadn't cracked open his sternum to find a secret stash of extra limbs and vital organs, so who knew? The clothes didn't seem to have any blood on them so someone must have stripped him or made him strip and slit his throat after. Or maybe he slit it himself after getting down to his skivvies in the fridge. His underwear, by the way, were those white atrocities men who never get fucked wear. They even had this bloke's name written in magic marker on them, like he was seven years old and his mother separated his wash from the rest of her lot for him. I bent down some more to try and read the name. It read: John.

I heard the freezer door open behind me and felt a hand around my throat before I saw the blade gleaming right next to my eye in the firelight. "Now you know," the kid said from behind me. "Don't try and fight. Just start walking backwards with me."

I did what he said, surprised he didn't just kill me. I should have kept quiet but I was too tired and beaten down from lack of dope and too many monsters. "So if that's the actual John Lopez who's a bellhop dogsbody at the hotel here, who might I have the pleasure?"

"Dude, what?"

I still liked this kid. "If you're not John Lopez, who the fuck are you? What's your real name?"

We got to the walk-in fridge door then stopped. "John, actually. Just one of those coincidences. Trippy, right?"

"Are you even Mexican then?"

"Mexican? Dude, I was never Mexican. I'm fucking Puerto Rican." He used one of his feet to kick the door open behind us. Light washed in.

"Anus, Ah-nus, what's the fucking difference?"

Tetrahex

The kid spun me around and herded me out into the kitchen in front of the others. Rikki was still too busy enjoying her first bit of meat in years to look up, but Marcus, still impressively in control of his facilities, assessed the situation right away and got up out of his chair holding his hands up. "Whoa, son, what's going on here?"

The kid's arm around my throat was tight, little shit was stronger than I would have thought. But his grip wasn't so tight that I couldn't bark, "Kid's not even a bellhop, the dead bellhop's in the icebox naked with his throat slit—" The kid pulled back and cut me off.

"Why was he naked?" At some point Rikki looked up from her meal.

"Fuck is wrong with you, woman?" Marcus said. "It's so the kid could wear his bellhop uniform and impersonate staff of the hotel."

"His name, however, actually is John," I blurted out. The kid tried to choke any more out of me. "...But not Lopez." For some reason I found this important information to share. "Also, not Mexican, did anyone else think that he was or was it just me?"

"Everyone quiet," the kid tried his best to sound menacing. Admittedly it was working even if you could hear him trying. "Look, no one here understands what's actually going on right now." Marcus opened his mouth to speak but the kid cut him off. "You think you do but trust me, you don't. You think you're going to get outside? That someone out there is going to help you? There's no one else who can save you. No one but this man." He shook me as punctuation. "I need to take him to the top of the hotel."

"Top of the hotel, sure. That makes sense," Rikki told him.

"Do not placate me, punk rocker," the kid said. Even Rikki didn't know how to respond to that. "Listen: the Alucinari Hotel was designed by Pedrik Navarj, a Darjmainian aristocrat and architect who was inspired by Robert Fludd, an English occult philosopher and astrologer and mathematician and cosmologist who died in the 1600s."

"Did you memorize all that from a book in school or something?" Rikki asked.

"Church actually," the kid answered.

"And he was homeschooled, remember?" I said.

"Oh right," Rikki said.

"Shut up," the kid told us. "My point about Fludd was that he was into a lot of different shit. Including this book about musical theory he wrote called *De Musica Mundan*. In that book, Fludd devised a mundane monochord and a celestial monochord and a divine monochord that linked up the Ptolemaic universe to musical intervals."

"…Well, everybody knows that," Rikki said.

"You're talking a music of the spheres type of thing, aren't you?" I said.

"Everything in the universe has a certain vibration, a frequency," the kid said. "You, me, the earth itself, everything. This building was built by Pedrik Navarj as one giant musical instrument to match and play along with the vibration of our world. At the top of the building there is a chamber where Codger can play this instrument which will reverberate through the body of the entire building."

So there it was. I was right all along. He was a nutter. Another Helter Skelter fucking loony. Another one like the Yank fucker who shot Lennon. He wasn't in league with the beasts outside. Just another loony hearing shit in the songs that wasn't there. It made me feel so hollow all of a sudden; that we spent so much time on our music and they either didn't pay attention at all to what we were trying to say or they got the message so turned around and twisted that needn't have bothered with it in the first place. He had killed already; if I didn't get away I'd either be dead by his hand or by whatever was waiting for us outside the door or in the lobby.

So I told him, "I'll do whatever you say, kid. I'll tell you all about what actually happened on the night that inspired the song, 'Frivolous Black.' I'll tell you all about the big black shape that loomed over me while I slept in bed." I eyed Marcus who lowered his brow to me ever so slightly. I returned the gesture as best I could. God, I hoped he was actually as sobered up as he appeared. "But you have to know that if we go out that door neither of us is going to be making it up to the chamber at the top floor, man." I couldn't see his face, of course, but I felt for a moment like I had got through to him. I don't know why I thought that, because the next thing I knew I caught the look on Rikki's face. She looked braced for something. And then Marcus lunged forward and the kid pulled back and he ran his blade against my left cheek. There was a sting as it cut the top layer of my skin and then I felt something unhinge itself inside my head.

Like a door split open inside my brain. That sudden relief of a tremendous pressure previously unknown to me but now obvious in its absence, that relief had returned. There was that sound again, like with Frankie, a buzz. A hiss. My last thought was simply, *Oh, it's me.* And then in a breath I was no longer myself.

No longer just I…

We…

We were so much more.

So many more.

No longer just human.

We were infinite.

And We didn't take kindly to knives cutting any of our faces.

Even if We had countless other faces.

The people in the kitchen, however, all shared one face, one of rapt horror at the beautiful new thing We had become.

Schizoid

We walked on many worlds. We wandered through stars and were lost in oceans of thought and galaxies of dreams. In one instant We were everywhere all at once. It was agony. It was madness. It was sublime. It was too much. It was also without beginning or end. We, not I anymore, We... We were a countless array of Codger Burtons. And We were much more than that too. Other versions of a similar mold, variations on a theme. Some not even human. Weird-limbed homesick nightmares as disgusted or enthralled by the human shape as the humans were by their natural forms. All of us lost in a howling wilderness of this vast, listless oblivion. Screams on a wind, unable to even tether ourselves on the ears of a merciless god. Less than ghosts, lower than demons, more like abandoned gods buried beneath the rubble of our children's fresh empire. We saw the worlds through our new countless eyes. We thought the same way. All at once, a complex cobweb, a circuit board gossamer, a snarl of information that weighed us down into incompetence or insanity. We enjoyed such pain because of this. But We also suffered such delight. For now We no longer felt the indignity, the vulgarity of the self. Of I. Solitude, privacy all myth now. Instead We basked in the hive. Countless beings connected by a vibration. A shared sound. A marker that chained them to one another across universes. And in many of these universes there were witnesses indigenous to each realm who cried out in terror at the sight of our birth. At the death of the form they had known to be who and what We were.

But back in the universe where Codger Burton was in the kitchen of the Alucinari Hotel with the kid, Rikki, and Marcus, Codger Burton had become something almost unspeakable. With a pair of our new eyes We could observe from behind our skull that the kid had dropped the knife he once held at our fragile singular cheek and was now recoiling and shrieking. In his eyes We registered his bland terror as our back became a rolling, ever shifting composite featuring our new litany of shapes. We cycled through limbs and organs, sinew and shell, fang, wing, carapace and feather, always becoming, never satisfied, never still. We were an open wound that never stopped bleeding. A mouthful of shipwrecked teeth gnashing ourselves to sinking splinters. A living kaleidoscope of stretching flesh, misshapen, swelling bone, and blossoming viscera. Naturally, the kid screamed. He fell to his knees, either in worship or abject horror. From our vantage point above there was no difference.

There was also no clear desire either. Nothing that one would recognize as a desire.

There was a hunger. Not for sustenance, not for knowledge. Something darker and older than that. It was the same thing that made babies cry out when being torn from the womb. Beyond fear, pain, or confusion. We were suffering and We wanted to share it. From the cluster of heads and wreath of eyes that were still to our front We saw Marcus at the barricade, trying to drag away the tables they'd placed there earlier. Tables We had helped drag in place back when We were still I. Marcus called out to Rikki to help him. But Rikki was busy.

She had a plastic bottle of cooking oil in one hand and a butane lighter in the other. She came towards us, ignored Marcus who continued to bleat at her, and she threw the oil on one of our faces. A nest of curled horns unpacked itself from where that face once occupied. It flowered out rapidly and then this latest head of ours thrashed forward, knocking the lighter from Rikki's grip and cutting and slashing her face and arms. She didn't fall, she stood her ground, with tears in her eyes she reached for her axe which she had placed on a nearby table. We thrashed again and caught her arm before she could use the axe. Her arm twisted beneath one of our spiraled horns and We threw her over the table with a quick twist of our neck. Marcus chased after her, abandoning his fruitless effort to move the barricade by himself.

As he helped her off the ground We spied from behind the boy, the kid still on his knees but now with hands raised towards us. Pleading or attempting to claw at us like some beast himself. We met this with more beasts of our own. Our back collapsed and out sprang another of our selves. This self flashed fluorescent and had hoofed heavy limbs which landed like hammers on the floor to the sides of the boy. Beneath him there was a small pool of urine and it felt warm against our new legs. But still he reached towards us. His eyes brimmed with tears. What could he want? More importantly, what did We want? The only thing We could want... Above him our gleaming beast face hung down to look at the boy's tears more closely. Still he reached up.

Elsewhere We were lost in the storm that shifts between worlds.

Elsewhere We were roaming through familiar cityscapes and old haunts.

Elsewhere We were passing across blood-red deserts with

strange stone cities populated with creatures who had as little knowledge of us as We them.

Elsewhere We were involved in innumerable other melees. Our fractured, mingled form viewed as a cancerous intrusion on reality itself by the different people and life forms unlucky enough to stand witness to our arrival. How they tried to destroy or run from us, to defend the narrow confines of what they had deemed reality. How each of these beings thought themselves master of this. What and what wasn't real. And how We stripped that mastery away from each and every one…

Elsewhere We were everywhere in one shared instant. And We were scattered into pieces. And We screamed and screamed and screamed with our countless throats. And this music was to be our only true company.

Back in the kitchen the boy finally touched our snout which hung above him and We opened the burning black mouth of our beast face. His arm disintegrated away inside our jaw clean. Only a small trickle of blood and the rest burnt down, cauterized just past his elbow leaving a bright blue stump. He flipped backward in a half cartwheel and landed painfully to the floor. His agony was high-pitched, hysterical. But his agony was nothing compared to our own. Our burning beast face consumed his charred limb. We could all taste the ash of his flesh and bone. On our other side Marcus and Rikki both had given up trying to fight us and had returned together to removing the barricade. We crawled toward them. Rikki looked back, eyes wide at the sight of us. She said something to us, trying to plead with the Codger Burton she knew but it made no difference. Each step for us was misery, each movement a punishing feat. Trying to get enough of us to focus on one place, on one world in the myriad we inhabited simultaneously, and on one concerted effort in that world; it was excruciating. Rikki kept talking. Only now her words were slightly clearer. They felt more impacting. Almost hypnotizing. From out of some of our eyes harsh yellow light began to pour upward. Building a structure for communication, a threat and an invitation. Rikki kept talking, she had stopped trying to move the table. Marcus, now flummoxed, reached over and slapped her across the face thinking she had gone mad. She punched him square in the balls in response and then began screaming what she was saying before to us. She never looked away from us even as the yellow lights and the cathedral it was constructing started to grow closer and closer to her head. Even as We pulled forward until We were right on top of her. She never looked away from us. She never looked away from…. me.

And then like a drill boring into my brain I could hear her. Every word. *"Bathe yourself in darkness, rinse with night. For the sun has made you dirty with its light."* Every last word. She wasn't saying anything. She was singing. And every word, every stupid fucking word was my own. She was singing my song to me.

And then in a breath We were no more and there was only me.

There was a crushing return of pressure, I remember Rikki, Marcus, and the kid all screaming, and then some sort of light, or maybe fire.

Then things went dark.

They stayed that way for quite some time.

Beyond This Sleepless Dream

June 8th, 1969, the night before I walked into band practice with a story that, along with the new guitar sound Vinnie came up with, changed all of our lives, and I thought I was asleep having a very vivid nightmare.

I've always thought it was just a nightmare. But now I could see it was no dream.

The story everyone knew was that I was reading a Crowley book, I fell asleep and then woke up to see some sort of black apparition. The "Frivolous Black," I called it 'cause it seemed to dance around, almost playfully, enticingly. Black because that's what it was: black, a living shadow. Vaguely in the shape of a person. Only its eyes showed any sort of color. And all they did was burn. The story goes I saw this thing in my room, I screamed, and then it disappeared. I went to band practice, told the others about the story, they laughed it off and then it was Sully who suggested I write some lyrics about the encounter for this new piece of music Vinnie showed us. This really scary sounding number built around an augmented version of the tritone from Gustav Holst's piece called "Mars." I had played it for Vinnie only the day before. I was getting into some classical stuff, not a lot, but some of it was all right.

Vinnie heard that part, the tritone, and it must have gave him ideas. The tritone was an augmented fourth. I remember trying to impress Vinnie with some music theory shit I had picked up from reading books about it. I told him, "Hear that real dark sounding bit that's playing, that's the augmented fourth. It's a dissonant interval." I had no idea at the time what that meant. "Lower numbers produce consonant harmonies and the higher the numbers, the more you get dissonance. So like the further you go away from one, the more you get away from harmony and the closer you get to the dissonance." He looked at me like I was speaking Martian. Which I was, I suppose, given the name of the song we were discussing. But really he could just tell I was full of shit. Just repeating what I had heard out of a book.

"It makes me want to shit in my shoes," Vinnie said. We laughed. He was right. It was an unsettling sound.

"The churches used to ban this tritone, called it 'The Devil's Chord.'" Vinnie just ran a hand through his goatee, sat there and let me bullshit him for a little bit longer.

That's the story everybody knew. It wasn't the truth but it sounded good. Paired with the lyrics detailing an encounter with a dark seductive shadow that offered some sort of Faustian bargain, it inferred to our audience that maybe this had really happened to me. Or to Sully, I suppose. Most of our crowd still thought he wrote all the words he was singing. What I had thought had actually happened was much simpler but also a fair bit more involved.

Simpler because it had all been a dream. I never woke up to watch my visitor vanish.

I just woke up hours later in the morning with the sun shining and all was well. More involved because it wasn't just a simple stare down with some fire-eyed demon and poof, he disappeared leaving me with a bostin' idea for a new song. No, it also wasn't like it was in the song. Nothing offered me any of my deepest desires in exchange for my immortal soul or any of that tripe. In my dream I woke and the shadow was hovering above me. Filling the room was a sort of buzz, a hum like a swarm of hornets. The visitor hunched over me and its eyes weren't eyes at all, just burning windows, portals into its head. And inside its head there was only burning. Like the inside of a sun, it was violent, radiant, a churning burning ocean. And within that ocean a broken melody more rapturous and heartbreaking than the secret name of god itself played in broken pieces on and off. Always being drowned out by the fire. I had never seen or heard anything so full of beauty and I couldn't turn away from it. The shadow had me. It didn't speak. There was no need. All was understood. There was no bargain. It would simply give me what I needed in order to find that song. To finish that music. To make it heard. I would do anything for this. It gave my life purpose. It gave my identity meaning. So the shadow produced a long thin arm and pointed sort of hand.

Resting in its palm was a large black seed. The shadow withdrew its hand and the seed remained in the air above me. My hands at my sides, I had risen to my knees on the bed waiting for the exchange. For my gift to be given. The seed moved through the air and entered my navel and then burrowed its way inside me.

I could feel long black branches growing inside me. Could sense the seed deep inside my center, and from deep inside it a strong thick trunk from which more branches would stretch out. I could feel their sharp tips and twigs scratching tenderly behind my eyes and their dark red leaves budding, wrapping and then enfolding over my brain.

Now, December 12th, 1980, I knew that was no dream. That visitor was the same as the creature I'd seen in the hotel lobby... The Earworm. I don't care what Marcus said, it was a fitting name. The story, the lie I had been telling all these years, had been closer to the truth than my actual memory. But now I remembered the truth. Not that it would do me much good. I was lost. I did not know where I was anymore or even if *I* was anymore but something told me that the tree planted inside me all those years ago had died. And that I was supposed to have had died with it.

Antigonish Stares

I woke up to find my own dead face staring right back at me. Nose to nose, right on top of me. Its eyes wide but listless, mouth agape like some dead animal hit by a lorry. This wasn't a mirror but an actual physically manifested reflection. A double. Or perhaps something worse; I went to feel my own face, to see if I had been skinned and whatever sick creature who did the carving had thought it a laugh to show me its handiwork, but I couldn't move my arms. The panic spread swiftly. *Trapped*, that one word my only thought. I struggled some more but I was wedged into something and it wasn't budging. I tried to calm myself. Was I really face to face with my own corpse? Yes, the moustache was a dead giveaway; second best in the band. But I was still failing to put it all together. Didn't matter, not yet, all that was important was that I get out of this. But I felt buried; I could wiggle my toes and fingers but to actually move my limbs seemed difficult. I wasn't bound, not exactly, but I was surrounded. It was hot in there, miserable hot like a fucking jungle. And the smell was unbearable. I used to work at an abattoir. This stunk like an abattoir that had a clam chowder soup kitchen in the middle of it. All around me I could feel soft and sometimes brittle lukewarm material, some of it sticky or wet. But I couldn't turn my head to investigate further. I was in the middle of something, felt like it was the thickest of treacle and my only view was my own dead face. This was rather confusing. I did, however, finally grasp that there was no way I had been skinned; my doppelganger above me was staring down at me. Which meant he had his eyes, which meant he didn't have mine because I was staring at him. This was incredibly comforting despite it making things infinitesimally even more perplexing.

I looked up at my own worn away face with its empty stare. I wasn't going to die here. Not like him. I put all of my strength in my right shoulder and my left leg and finally managed to lurch myself free. Then I started digging, which felt more like swimming. The only way to go was up so I had to push into my handsome friend hanging above me. When we brushed foreheads our lips met and before I could laugh or scream about it a generous amount of saliva poured out of his jostled jaw and into mine. I coughed and cursed and spat as I pushed on past him. I decided I needed to quit smoking on top of the booze and coke too. Everything in my twin's mouth tasted of ash and ranch dressing. No wonder my wife left me. Once I got past my own dead face I found that's all it was: Just my head. No attached body. As I squeezed past him I looked down and saw him turned around now looking back up at me. One eye shut, a wink for my nudge. Now that all my limbs had become liberated I started thrashing them upward full force. I had to get out. Had to breathe. I pushed myself up on my hands and forced my way through a crack in the surface of whatever I was stuck in. Fresh air, at least fresher air, filled my nostrils and my mouth and I saw the familiar glow from off one of the jug lanterns. The fucker still hadn't died. I was still in that kitchen. And I was alone. I popped my left shoulder up through the opening then worked the arm out too. I finally got my last foot free and slid down the skin I was now laying on top of. I wasn't alone, not really. I still hadn't escaped the We it seemed…

There it was, my prison, the hot trap I had burrowed out of like some desperate hairless gopher. A pile of dead mes. At least most of them looked like me, the ones that looked human at all. All of them were incomplete, many were just parts. All of them were jammed together, compressed down into one sort of being. A composite corpse. Arms sprang from torsos or heads, tongues sagged down out of eye cavities or around necks like scarves. There was one back that looked more like rhinoceros skin and along its thick grey surface rippled hundreds of small white spikes. I looked closer and saw that they were all upside down human teeth, the big four-pronged fuckers in the back of the mouth and the thinner canines and front teeth which always looked like great big white corn kernels to me. They had all grown out of this skin upside down, completely useless but sort of beautiful if you went for that sort of thing. There were also some other limbs I had no accounting for. Mandibles, claws, tails, horns, or maybe just protruding ribcages. Nestled throughout this pile were my own faces. Some looked just like the bloke who greeted me in the bathroom mirror every morning and some looked a bit different. Fatter, skinnier, some with no moustaches—these were easily the most wretched of the lot. There were a few other human faces that weren't me but I still felt a sort of kinship to them for some reason. And the same sort of, for lack of a better word, embarrassment, of seeing them or myself like this. Some of them were women. One even looked remarkably like my own mom in the photos I'd seen when she'd been younger. It was odd—obviously it was odd, it was a pile of eviscerated mes and monster mes, that's fucking abnormal—but what was really odd was the feeling I got looking at all of them. Must have had at least seventeen or twenty faces in there, god knows how many different limbs and other parts. I looked at them and got that feeling you get when you see a photo of yourself or hear your voice on a recording and you hated it. Just loathed it outright.

Why? Not just because you looked fatter than you thought you looked, or your voice was squeakier or more annoying sounding than you thought… You hated these reflections of you because they did not seem like you. Like the way you thought of yourself. They were at odds with the delusion you'd made of yourself. We forget that everything we experience is tainted by our viewpoint, especially the way we experience ourselves. I looked at the gallery of my own dead faces, that was what I really was or could be and I didn't like it one bit.

Because now I was me again and from this seat I had no use for the dead truth piled up in front of me.

I was also naked. And for some reason I felt a little shy having all those mes staring at my equipment. Even if some of them were monsters mes and all of them were dead mes. I was not comforted either by the idea that these other mes probably had similar equipment to my own back when they were alive and still attached to said equipment. It still felt like sharing too much. I didn't want to consider what the monster mes had been hiding in their trousers before we got compacted in together. Then again maybe what they were packing was lying in the pile too. I suppose I just didn't recognize monster genitalia when I saw it. Who would? One thing I did notice was that most of the bodies in the pile looked dried up, like husks. Like something had drained them, stole the life right out of them. I felt great conversely. Now that I was out from under all that dead weight I felt like my old self again. Like my old old self. I felt like I used to back in the good old days. Back when the band was young and playing music was still a good time and not an actual job. And the pressure I had felt before become part of whatever I had become part of, that pressure was back but I welcomed it. It didn't feel so much like a burden now, more like a helpful tether or a welcome weight that kept me from slipping away.

But there was no one to share these revelations with. The kitchen was deserted. Where the kid had been, where he had reached out and I, or We, had burnt off his arm, there was only a bit of blood on the floor. The barricade had been moved, just enough to let Rikki and Marcus squeeze out. Presumably while I folded in on my multiple selves, or imploded, or whatever the hell had occurred. I still didn't remember it all. It was there in my mind but so was a sort of block. I could feel it weakening the longer I was conscious. But it still hadn't fallen away entirely. I put it on the backburner and decided to focus on more important things. Namely, that if Rikki and Marcus were still out there I had to find them.

Tell them I was feeling better now, that I was sorry for monstering out before and all that, and I really wanted to be wearing pants when I did this. That was, of course, if they were still alive and the Earworm hadn't gotten to them first. I still wasn't sure what exactly it wanted from me. The most logical answer was what the kid had said all along; it wanted to come back and collect. Pick up that seed it put into me. But I couldn't shake that this didn't feel right. There was something more, something I was still missing.

Swinging an axe naked with my balls slapping around this way and that is possibly the manliest I'd ever felt as well as the most terrified. I chose not to think this coincidence. The axe was left by Rikki, I'm guessing she and Marcus left in quite the hurry whilst I was doing my origami routine. I swung the axe again and broke off another of the locks. I was going through the staff lockers in a backroom of the kitchen. Hoping to find someone's change of clothes that I could use. The first two lockers left me with a chef's coat and a pair of chef clogs that'd fit okay. But I'd still like some sort of pants if I was going to face certain death, it just seemed the proper way to go about things. Locker three was the jackpot. A pair of blue jeans that would work well enough and a big thick fridge coat with an attached hood.

For the first time since I woke up things were looking likewise. It hit me then how up I was feeling in general. Almost like I'd just done a small mountain of snow white up my nose and the girls were waiting in the wings after a show telling me they'd another beautiful place for me to shove my face. I had been feeling this spark since I crawled my way out of the pile of husks and their viscera. And I had music in my head too. Not exactly like I was hearing it, but whispers of it, sketches of what it should be. It was the old feeling, back when Friv used to go down to the room and work on our material. We all had ideas, most of which weren't even really half-formed but we had this trust, this faith, this certainty that the minute we plugged in, the rest would just come pouring out of us as natural as the sun coming up in the morning. The minute Vinnie would drop his riff we'd be right there locked in with our own parts. I'd asked Vinnie a few times if he wrote those riffs on his own before band practice. And he always said some variation of, "Yeah, but not really." Or, "I do but it all changes, gets turned around or just completely rearranged when we're all together making it into a proper Frivolous tune." That was the feeling I had. I needed to get my instrument, I needed to get a pad of paper. I had words, I had sounds, music practically screaming to be released from me.

But there was no time. And the only instrument I could

think of was whatever madness the kid was going on about while he held a knife to my throat. The room, the chamber at the top of the hotel. Some sort of music room, built by an old mad Darjmainian. It sounded like occult bollocks and besides, I had more pressing concerns. I threw the clothes on as fast as I could. The second locker I had opened was still ajar and I noticed a small boom box lying in there I must have glossed over initially. I turned it on, just trying to see if the weather had cleared up at all, or if there were any reports of strange monsters that resembled album covers eating people or whatever. Nothing. Nothing came in at all. No crackle. Not even dead air. Nothing. The Earworm, I was certain this was its doing. Like with the red light it used to control the lift back with Frankie. As I was making my way out the jug lantern's light dipped again then finally died. The room went black and I got the sudden fear that all the dead and discarded pieces of me left on the floor were going to reassemble themselves and come for me in the dark. Take me to pieces and return me to their patchwork prison. Now was a good time to get out of there. There was a bit of light from the hole in the barricade so I followed it out of the black room.

I crept out of the hole looking like some renegade sous chef, or maybe a rather dainty Viking. I held my axe at the ready and tried to move quickly but carefully towards the lobby. The dim light I followed was coming from the hallway towards the lobby entrance. As I moved along the song I was hearing kept moving through my mind and making me almost giddy at the prospect of creating something new. I had to strain to keep from smiling. Which was fucking yampy but the truth. I was waiting for the boogeyman to come rip my head off and I was beaming like a kid on Christmas Eve going to bed early. I continued moving through the hallway looking for any signs of a struggle and finding none. Maybe the Earworm had moved on. Maybe Rikki and Marcus had made it out with no opposition. Maybe the kid did too... Then I remembered that little nutter pulling a blade on me. And the dead man in the freezer, the real John Lopez. The light coming up from the lobby, which was still quite weak, was now just up ahead. I looked behind me, tried to steady my breathing and balance the axe in case I needed to swing it. The air felt chilly as I rounded the next corner.

At the lobby waiting to greet me was yet another mystery. To the far left the doors leading outside were ajar and a tunnel was dug and burnt out, presumably with the little crème brûlée torches, just like Marcus had said. Snow was blowing in from the tunnel, pushed in by the wind outside which I could again hear howling. The weak light I had followed was a ring of sunlight that was coming out of the tunnel and resting on the marble floor in a halo. The mystery wasn't any of that. That all made some sort of sense. I followed the snowflakes dancing in the air and across the marble floor of the lobby as they landed atop the mystery. A body. Face down, wearing black, lying near the entrance of one of the elevators. It didn't look like any of the other three, and I should have been smarter but I was sick of not knowing all the angles, so I walked over to get a better look. I almost reached down and turned the body over with my hand until my brain started working again and I used the handle of my axe to poke at the body. Nothing stirred. The cold air blew against my hair and managed to part the curtains in back enough to kiss the back of my neck as I stared down to look some more at the body. I poked again, harder this time. When there was no reaction I gave it a full on jab. Still nothing. I placed my left hand on the shoulder of the body and held the axe at the ready with my right. If there was going to be any surprises I would be prepared with my own. The body was lighter than it should have been, felt more fragile too, and when I turned it over I saw that it was the witch. The mystery woman from the self-titled album cover. I could see up close she really didn't have eyes. Just dark recesses, spooky nooks that crawled back into her skull where the eyes should have been held with muscle and tissue. She looked just like the album cover, like an exact recreation of an old photograph. Grainy, indistinct, colors saturated, unreal looking. I rested the handle of my axe on the floor and peered down to get a better look at her lack of eyes and the strange texture of her skin. The wind picked up some more and I took its advice and shot back upright, bringing the axe down right through the witch's neck. She did not suddenly gasp when I took her head from her neck. Her arms did not raise, her fingers did not claw at me from beyond death's cold grip. There was not even blood. She was lifeless, beyond being already dead. She wasn't human in the slightest. From the stump of her neck and head I could see torn strands of material, yellow and grey, spilling out. It looked like the inside of a fruit that had been halved, like a melon. But not human, not even animal. She was just some sort of puppet, discarded after she failed to convince her intended audience. I wondered what became of the veined cobwebs she created earlier. I saw no remnants of them anywhere in the lobby. I had no idea how long I had been out; an hour, five, a whole day?

No, the jug lantern was still lit up when I woke so it couldn't have been a whole day. But if Rikki and Marcus had made it outside why hadn't anyone come to rescue or destroy me? I kicked the witch's head just to be sure, I was really liking these chef's clogs, and then I turned back to the tunnel. Maybe it was best that I didn't run into them again. How was I going to convince them I was okay again? How was I even sure I was okay? I mean, I felt great… I never feel great. I wasn't even thinking about the bottle at all. I wasn't myself, something had changed. I had changed. Maybe I would just transform again when I saw them. Maybe it was better to just get out and get away…

A glow started trickling into the room from up above. Red, neon, but faint like Christmas lights dying of cancer. I tilted my head up and saw something wondrous. A map of intricate glowing rivers arranged in the shape of a human hung above me. A circulatory system floating on its own and taking its fashion cues from Las Vegas. It lowered into the room through the ceiling, passed through it like a phantom. As it got closer I could see that where its eyes should have been sat empty glowing nets and these were not aimed in my direction. It didn't seem to notice me at all. Which was a small relief. Then it let out a moan that filled the entire room. It had that same compacted choir of a voice I had heard when I was We. Pain, pleasure, suffering, and salvation all stirred together into a thick, burning sound. It would have passed right through me I'm sure, but I stepped back out of the way and let it continue down through the floor and, I assume, eventually all the way into the earth. It moaned again once it was out of sight. I could hear the sound coming up through the ground.

Storm Mouth

Once I got outside I knew everything was wrong. The wind whipped the snow into a hissing fury that blinded me as I walked away from the tunnel into the wall of white. The sun was still up but you wouldn't know it. And it wasn't going to last much longer. I looked around, trying to shield my eyes so I could steal a glimpse of where I was going. Nothing, the wind and snow had left me completely snowblind and I could only see the faintest of dark outlines where the surrounding buildings stood. I looked down and saw two pairs of footprints in the snow. At least there was that. I followed them but already had a bad feeling. Something was off.

Nothing felt safe. All that elation I had been granted after emerging from the undertow of the We was gone now. Fear was all I felt. Which was fine, it'd make a good compass. But I couldn't figure out why exactly I was so afraid. I was outside, even if the city was deserted and it was a few miles to a hospital or fire station or the police; I was safer now, wasn't I? Closer to getting there at least? I couldn't shake it; I didn't like it out here. Nothing felt right.

I don't believe in precognition, tarot or any of that yampy nonsense but I will say I usually have a good sense of when things are about to turn shit. I had a terrible feeling the day we finally decided to sack Sully, for instance. We had been trying to record our follow up to the steaming pile that had been our last record and Sully kept ducking the sessions. He showed up one week, did a small mountain range of blow and when we finally forced him to stand behind the mic he took out his pecker and pissed on the lyrics I had written for him to sing. I wasn't particularly proud of the song in question but I went into the recording booth anyways and gave him a black eye before he could get his dick back in his pants. He just laughed and fell down on the wet spot on the floor. I still remember the sight of him there, lying in his own filth with those pages filled with my piss-stained words sticking to him like a blanket of newspapers sticks to a vagrant. And Sully, he just laughed and laughed.

Still, despite that it wasn't my decision to axe him. It was, but I wasn't the first one to bring it up. Vinnie did. Vinnie was our leader. He set the pace. And he said plainly what we all knew: Sully was never going to start working on this record and if we didn't make a new record soon we, as a musical entity, were dead. Punk was proving itself more than just a fad. And even in the world of heavy metal, the world that we built, we were being eclipsed. We had toured with this new American outfit that same year; they were tremendous. At least their guitarist was; he was like a new Hendrix almost. Incendiary, every night. He made the guitar sound like classical music played by a goddamn cyborg. It was unreal. It was so good people even overlooked the fact that the lead singer of this group couldn't carry a tune if he had a forklift. Though the fucker could do the splits off the drum riser and that was genuinely impressive. Well, these goddamn Yanks, they blew us off the stage every single night. And they were supporting their debut. No one knew a fucking word of any of their songs but they'd be

screaming along by the last chorus. And us? We were supporting the worst thing we as a unit ever produced. And Sully
was a buffoon on stage at this point. Just a disgrace. Even our
old material now sounded so half-hearted and uninspired that
we might as well have lip synced and mimed it. One night
this Yank band, they covered "Tetrahex," I honestly think they
meant it as a compliment. The crowd went off their head. Off
to the side of the stage me and Vinnie and Sully watched them
as they played. I could see the defeat on Vinnie's face. He was
thinking the same as me: *Why can't that be us anymore?* And
then I looked at Sully. He was banging his head along. "What's
this tune? Fucking bostin' it is. That guitar player is flash, isn't
he?" We kicked the Yanks off the remainder of the tour two
nights later.

That's when it first entered into my head that this thing with
Sully was coming to a head. So I wasn't the least bit surprised
after the incident in the recording booth when Vinnie told me
we needed to get rid of Sully. Nor was I surprised when Burt,
Sully's mate from back in primary school, agreed with Vin.
Which left it up to me. And it should have been an easy decision. I loved Sully, I did, but he was self-destruction incarnate.
In fact in a band full of sticks of a dynamite he was a goddamn
hand grenade. But, what would we be without him? What
would my words be without him to sing them? And yet there
wasn't really any choice, there was no way to work with him
anymore. Even if we just toured and didn't record anything
new, became a purely nostalgic act there was no life in the
live act anymore either. So I said Sully was out too. And that's
when the other two asked if I'd be the one to break it to him.

Vinnie couldn't do it because he was always throwing Sully out of the group and Sully was always telling Vinnie that
he quit. So it wouldn't mean anything if Vinnie cast him out

again. Burt couldn't fire him on account of the primary school history and being so close to Sully; he used that to duck the Judas card and I didn't really blame him. I'd have done the same if I could. But no, it had to come from me. That's what would make it real. I woke up that day knowing I'd have to do it, and my stomach was a knot. I finished a bottle of red wine by myself, snorted an entire Christmas village and then I went to Sully's flat to go and break the news to him. His girl opened the door and told me he was at the studio waiting for us. I told her this was our day off, it was Sunday, we weren't scheduled to record then. So she got suspicious and closed the door on me muttering to herself about what little bitch had gotten her claws into Sully this time. I got to the studio about an hour later and one of the blokes who worked there told me that sure enough Sullivan had been there but now he was gone. Said he waited around for a few hours and then said he was going to the pub.

I went to a few of his usual haunts but never found him. So I called his flat again at the end of the night. Sully was back, miraculously, his bird was in the back admonishing him for some perceived, though quite likely extramarital transgression, and I could barely hear him so he told me to hold on and then he took the phone into the toilet. He was drunk and high, but so was I, and no more than was customary for us at the time so I decided to tell him how it was. And like a lot of things in life, the big moments, the ones that decide how everything else is going to shake out, it wasn't dramatic at all. All the parties involved seem to know what was coming so there was really no fight. Nothing was truly a surprise. Sully got quiet and I asked him if he had heard me. And he said, "Yeah, mate. Yeah." I asked him what he was going to do and he laughed. "Don't worry about me, I've still my voice, I still got my face.

What are you lot going to do?" The way he said it wasn't exactly catty or mean-spirited; which made it worse. There was
enough genuine concern for me and the remaining group that
it cut me much worse than if he was just trying to get a rise out
of me. Because he was right. What band had ever survived the
loss of their singer? We ended the conversation cordially. He
said, "Cheers, Codger. I love you." Then he hung up.

The next day we were in the studio and I told Vinnie and
Burt and we talked about next moves. About finding a new
singer. Whether or not we wanted to scrap all the material we
had been working on already and start fresh. I was in favor of
this. I suspected part of the reason Sully wasn't cooperating
these sessions was due to the material being so lackluster. As
we talked there was a sense of loss but also excitement at what
might lie ahead for us. We did a lot of blow that night. Had a
lot to drink. And we spoke about how good it was to get that
loose cannon Sully out of the group. He was always getting
wasted, he was unreliable. We couldn't trust him to finish anything. Of course we didn't record anything that day ourselves,
I shudder now to think how much each day in that studio cost
us. As the night went on it I started to see our giddiness for
our new future as more and more us trying convince ourselves
that we still had one. At least from my end that's what I think
I was doing. Someone invited some birds over at some point
and we had a damn going away party for Sully without him
there. Eventually through the haze of it all and just as we were
preparing to leave for the night to continue the celebration
one of the engineers told me he had something he thought I
should hear. I followed him to the control deck and he played
a reel. "This is from last night."

"Okay, new tune, take one." It was Sully. He was singing a
take of the new song, the one with the lyric he had pissed all

over the day before. And it wasn't the best song in the world, much of that I was to blame. But he sang it well, and with conviction. He gave it his all, you could hear it on the tape. And when he was finished with his part and as the song continued on with a guitar solo that we would have eventually put a fade out on I could hear him talking to the engineer. "Sounds good, doesn't it? Fucking love this one. Love these words. Codger blows my mind with these things, he does." I realized then that Vinnie and Burt had joined me at some point to hear what was playing. No one said anything. We didn't discuss giving Sully another chance but we didn't go out with the girls and everyone else to continue the celebration as planned either. We just went home and said nothing to one another. I drank some more and passed out. Soon after was when I tried to get clean for the first time. That song, by the way, we scrapped my words and Sully's vocal and gave it to the American imp. He renamed it "Weeping Wizard." It sounds like "Leaping Lizard" the way he sings it. I don't remember what it was called when Sully sang it anymore. I was too fucked up when I had written it to recall and he had, after all, pissed on my only notes.

Outside now I kept on the trail for another five minutes or so when I saw some lights in the distance. Snow plow or fire engines. My fear slunk away and I started running towards the lights. They were moving closer to me too. Two vehicles, still couldn't tell what kind but there were two pairs of headlights heading my way. Even the wind was beginning to die down. When one of the headlights moved away from the other in its pair I told myself they must have been four-wheelers. Then one of the lights flew up into the air fifty feet or so and I stopped running. The wind died down completely and gave me a glimpse of what the lights were attached to. I started running off to the right, hoping to find something to hide behind. The lights were part of some kind of animal. Each light was a teardrop-shaped bioluminescent appendage suspended on the end of a fleshy growth that hung out and forward from each creature's back. Like giant anglerfish, only they could fly. I don't know if the things in the air spotted me but I was guessing my dark fridge coat made me an easy target in the middle of all this snow so I took it off. The chef's jacket I was wearing was dirty as a dish after dinner but it was still white and not dark. I looked back to see if the things with the light were following and that's when I caught my first real look at the city: Protruding from the earth stood cragged towers that looked like bone or tusk, there were hundreds of them, maybe more, as far as the eye could see. They were big as buildings, some dark grey but covered partially in snow, others as white as the snow itself. They stretched on with no end in sight. They sprung from the ground straight but started to curl and twist like ram's horns as they neared their tops up in the sky. This wasn't Boston; I wasn't sure if it was even Earth. I had looked out at it when I had woken up in my hotel room and not given it a second thought because of the snow storm.

In between some of these crooked pillars I saw more lights. Swimming in the air like schools of fish. Some of these schools were headed in my direction. I looked around frantically, waiting for the things that the lights grew out of to come into hideous view. I could hear a sound. It wasn't the wind, it was unlike anything I'd ever heard before. It must have meant they were close. But then the wind came back, and with it the snow in my eyes. Through the din of the storm I could still hear the new strange sound of the lights and they sounded closer. I prepped my axe, ready to swing at anything that came near. The sound of them rushed closer; was it the sound of them moving through the air? Or was it a howling of some kind?

Screaming like a pack of wolves in the hunt. I gripped down on the axe, my back teeth clenched so hard I thought they'd crack. This time the sound was accompanied with a flash of light maybe twenty feet from me, swimming in the air. Then the snow came on hard and obscured it from view, but I knew it was still coming right for me. I heard the sound— I swung my axe and something screamed, *"Jesus."* There was no shock of impact, I didn't hit anything, but there was a flash of light and now I could see what I was swinging at... Marcus. He stood back like he had just backed out of the way of my swing. I noticed some pieces of color seemed to be falling out of his midsection. Dark blue, the same color as his coat. I didn't see any blood so I must have just nicked his coat. Thank god. He looked terrified. I wasn't sure if it was of me or not. Behind him was Rikki, she was charging towards us, same look on her face and then I could see her motivation following close behind. Behind her were the lights, only a few paces out of step. The sound they made took whatever Rikki screamed next with it. I turned around and ran. I heard Marcus behind me doing the same.

I was running back towards the hotel, I knew nothing else. At some point Rikki had overtaken my lead and started leaving Marcus and me behind. "Come on," she yelled back. I tried to keep up but damn that girl was fast. It occurred to me then that she was probably yelling at Marcus and not me. All around us I could hear the sound of them. Their light washing over the sides of my vision. The need to turn around and see how close they were, and what they actually really were, was nearly impossible to quell. But I couldn't risk turning my head even a little and then running into something or tripping. Besides, it was getting hard to make out Rikki's coat in all the flurry. It was getting hard to see the hotel too. If I lost her or it what was I going to do? Then my foot sunk into the snow and sent me to the ground and Marcus right into me as I went. There was some sort of hill and we were rolling down it together screaming. In the tumble the tip of my axe cut into my arm just above the triceps. The pain was sharp and sudden and it was accompanied with fear: I was cut before when I changed, was it going to happen again? The sting of it almost made me let go of the weapon as well but I thought better of that. If I lost that axe I might as well have left the hotel naked when I came out here. Our momentum stalled and finally me and Marcus hit bottom. I could see some of my blood pouring out of my sleeve but my arm still worked so it couldn't have been too bad. I focused, tried to remain as calm as possible. Behind us the lights passed over the top of the hill we had just rolled down. The dark bramble of its tendrils flickered rapidly in the air as it soared over.

"Get up now," I yelled at Marcus who was already trying to get to his feet.

"Fucking tell me to get up, I'm up." We started running again and for a moment all I could see was the storm. White swishing this way and that like I was caught inside the television on a channel that didn't come in. I couldn't find the hotel, I couldn't find Rikki. The thing above us made its whishing, screeching sound again. "Codger, Codger," Marcus yelled to my left. There was the hotel and Rikki was almost to the front where the tunnel entrance waited. But she wasn't alone. Above her a black shape wreathed in light was coming right down on her. Framed against the white and the gold of dusk it appeared like some great burning bat in the sky. Next to its size Rikki was a lone field mouse. I was going to call out but then it was too late. The shape engulfed her. We were close, still running towards her, but I couldn't see Rikki anymore. Just the strange stringy limbs of the thing thrashing frantically. Its light suddenly pulsated out and it made its sound again just as we came up close to the thing. I was blinded by the pulse. Like getting out of a limo and the cameras started their snapping, and here was I without my sunglasses. But I didn't stop moving. The thing continued to scream and as my eyesight returned in flashes all I could make out was the writhing mass of it and what looked like fire. It was on fire. I could see Rikki now, she had her lighter out and was spraying some aerosol can in the direction of the beast, creating a flamethrower. Fucking bostin'! I didn't know what part of the thing was its head, if it even had a head, but whatever part was doing all the screaming was doing so because it was aflame. The light on the end of its lure blinked on and off then started to dim. It was hurt, maybe even dying. As I stood admiring the misshapen beast and its death rattle some part of it hit me hard in the chest. I don't know whether it was a tail or a wing or whatever those phalange things were but something thrashing fast without control took the wind right from me and I curled up and fell to my knees.

I tried to calm myself, forget about not being able to breathe. Hold my axe up, at least shield myself from another blow. Looking down at the blood river painting my sleeve didn't help matters. Neither did the feeling that something was wrong internally. Was it in my head or was something going to change with me again? I felt threatened, that's how I felt before... Was I being pulled back into the We? I saw some more fire and forgot about it. Marcus had his own aerosol can and lighter and he used it to burn the nearest black wing of the beast. The flame cast Marcus' roaring face in a hellish glow and I wondered if Vietnam wasn't far from his mind now. The light on the creature dimmed again and then that was it, it took to the sky and clumsily started swimming away into the air. With it being on fire and all it made me think of a comet that had come whizzing down into earth, then decided it didn't care for the place and turned around and promptly fucked off back the way it came. I could sympathize.

And I could breathe again. But I couldn't shake the fear that it might happen again, that I might change again and soon. I started to get up off my knees when I noticed the fire hadn't been put away yet. Standing above me were Rikki and Marcus.

"Don't move," Marcus said almost gently. Both held their torches out in opposing directions and looked down at me. I could see it in their eyes, the searching. Evaluating, judging, hoping, fearing. Could I blame them? But it was getting cold sitting on the ground bleeding.

"...What do you need me to say?"

Marcus gave me a long look. His eyes were black dots, told me nothing. "Did you know before? What you were, what you are?"

"No, and I don't think I am anymore."

"Don't think?"

"How can I be sure if I didn't know previously?"

"Did Frankie know?" Rikki asked. I gripped my axe.

Marcus looked down, his eyes black dots, nothing more. "I don't think Frankie knew either..." Marcus said. "Sorry, Codger."

"Wait."

"...see you when we get back to the world."

"Wait."

"Sorry."

"WAIT!"

They pressed down on the aerosol can levers and the fire came for me. I had one thought: *I have a song to play. A song to write. A song that could only come from me. And no one will ever hear it.*

But the fire never touched me.

The heat of it kissed my face but then quickly pulled back and away. And then up... the fire went up into the air. Marcus and his fire disappeared behind the mass of writhing black wings and strange glistening barbs and phalanges which dragged them up into the sky.

I was relieved. Not just to still be alive but because the weird limbs that claimed Marcus were not my own.

Grave Expectations

The thing dropped him back down to the ground a moment later. It did this from a height of twenty feet or so. Then it scooped Marcus up again, flew a little higher, and dropped him again. Repeat. Marcus made two sounds each time. His screaming, unending screaming, as well as the crunch and snap of his bones breaking and popping out of his skin with each new crash. When it brought him back up the fourth time, Marcus' scream had given way to a steady sob. I'm ashamed to admit I would have rather heard the scream. I wasn't watching him or the thing with the light that had him anymore, I was busy trying not to get put in a similar situation. Or to be burned alive looking like some sort of heretic chef. Rikki had turned her flame off the second the thing snatched Marcus and now she was trying to figure out how to help him. Poor kid still thought she could help him. She alternated between staring up in the air aiming her aerosol and her lighter at the ready but not firing because the thing was always too close to Marcus, and running to wherever it dropped his smashed, bloody body, hoping to get to him before it did. She was lost. It had happened to me earlier in the kitchen, bound to happen to anyone with this sort of shit. She was in shock. Which was good for me I suppose, since she was no longer trying to incinerate me, but as I made my way to the tunnel leading into the hotel I looked back and saw more of the lights swimming towards her in the nearly dark sky. Another thud and crunch announced that poor Marcus had been dropped again. The thing was toying with him the way killer whales do with those poor screaming seals they volley back and forth like tennis balls. Like a gull dropping a razor clam from on high repeatedly until it cracked so it could feast on the soft tissue within. I could still hear Marcus whimpering softly on the ground and Rikki still wasn't moving. She stood ten feet or so away from him with her hands in the air doing nothing but being easy prey.

The lights were all around us now. If I was going to get out of there I needed to leave. "Rikki, you thick-headed bitch, move your tits if you wish to keep them." She didn't move. The lights came close. I put my hand into the snow, took a handful of the stuff, packed it with the other hand and lobbed it at the side of her head. She turned away from Marcus still lying on the ground. Tears streaked her cheeks. "We have to go, love." She ran towards me. Behind her the thing came back for Marcus and took him away, still weeping, up into the near dark. Another of the things landed between Rikki and me with a detonation of sound. I swung the axe, lashing again and again at whatever part of it was moving towards me. A burst of flame erupted behind the beast and set its backside on fire. Rikki came darting around the right side of it still wielding the fire and for a moment I was afraid she'd turn it on me again. But she either had a change of heart or was too preoccupied to give it another go. Two more of the things touched down. One Rikki put the fire to immediately, but the other snarled in its syrupy voice and charged towards us, taking my foot in its grip. I lost my footing and was turned upside down when it started moving us up, dragging me off the ground. Up into the air where it'd start playing with me like they'd done to Marcus, until I cracked apart. I swung my axe again and again. After the first three whacks I stopped being afraid of cutting into my own foot and just swung blindly. Luckily I didn't hit myself but I also didn't cut through the beast. Red blood was oozing out from its feelers but it still had me tight in its grip.

"Give me your hand." Rikki was below me but I didn't think I could reach her. I stretched my left hand and my fingers were at least a foot away from her own. I swung again with the axe, cutting into the creature. Blood shot out in a wild torrent but still it climbed up in the air. And again, like before, I thought of my song. My little song that I wanted to share. That I wanted to make. I thought of it and it alone and I pulled my axe out of its skin and held it down just below the blade so Rikki could reach the handle. She took it and started pulling. The creature couldn't lift up any further with our combined weight, but Rikki wasn't quite strong enough to drag me out of its grip either.

"Give me the fire," I told her. She pulled down on the handle as hard as she could, pulling us down just a little bit closer, buying her some time so when she let go with her other hand and the creature regained its pull in this tug-o-war its recovery wouldn't be so lopsided as to destroy Rikki's entire share. She took her hand away and I felt myself being carried away again. She handed me the aerosol can and the lighter. My fingers were greasy and I felt the lighter slip away, but I caught it before it fell to the ground. There was a flash of light and I heard another creature close by, probably angling to get a piece of Rikki, and the thing that had a hold of me roared at it. For an instant it stopped trying to drag me up, distracted by this newcomer, and I took the lighter in my hand and started spraying the aerosol can. A wet slap of olive oil spray hit me in the nose and mouth and I turned the can around and thanked Christ I had tried the can first and not the lighter followed by the can. I hit the lighter and the whole beast went up like a roman candle. It dropped along with me and we both fell on Rikki and the new creature that had joined the fray. The burning beast rolled around in the snow, either trying to put out the fire or simply because it was mindlessly in pain. Either way this scared the other one enough that it took to the air and left me and Rikki to finally make our exit into the tunnel. We scrambled in, her first and me right after. I still had the can and the lighter and kept turning back ready to blast anything that followed. We got to the door of the hotel and into the lobby without any trouble. "Where to now?" I asked.

"No fucking idea. You were a monster, you know how they think, right? Where should we hide?"

"I wasn't... I guess I was but it doesn't work like that." Something heavy hit the ground in the tunnel. I looked at Rikki and she turned around and started heading towards the stairs. I could hear the thing in the tunnel getting closer. I liked Rikki's idea so I started running after her.

Remote Guidance

We were making our way to the third floor, using the crème brûlée torches to guide us when Rikki started talking; it had been a lovely exercise until that point. "So what the hell are you? A monster that's been pretending to be a wanker? A wanker who got turned into a monster? Or a wanker who got turned into a monster and then somehow got turned back into a wanker?" Before I had the chance to answer, "And where the fuck are we? Are we not on Earth anymore? Is that what this is? Fucking aliens? That's just perfect. I mean it made more sense when I thought it was demons."

"Did it?"

She was whispering all of this but also sort of whisper screaming it so I did the same. It sounded like my folks when they'd be in a row outside my bedroom door trying to keep it quiet to spare me, my brother and sister. It just made them sound angrier actually but it was also a bit of a laugh. Ahead of me Rikki rounded the corner and I tried to keep up. "Kind of. I never believed in aliens but I did believe in the devil… at least when I was younger. Thanks to stupid scary shit like your first record."

I thought of her back in the kitchen, when I wasn't myself, and her singing my own words back to me. "…What made

149

you… before, you started singing my song back to me, why? What made you think to do that?"

She turned around. Up close with all her black makeup smudged and running down her cheek I could see how young she really was. Twenty-four at best. Maybe ten years younger than myself, and my last ten years had felt like two lifetimes. "I don't know exactly. I was in shock and you looked… it was… I wasn't thinking. I just wanted to reach you… if you were still in there. I was singing it before I knew what I was doing."

"Thank you. It worked."

"Why did it, you don't mind me asking?"

"…Those lines. They were an old bit of poetry I wrote back before I had even joined the band. Years later I put 'em to music. But they still always felt like they were mine. Just mine, you know what I mean?"

She nodded slightly. "It was my favorite song, you know?"

"'Visitation Rites,' yeah?"

"Yeah, back before you went to shit." I grinned and we kept moving up.

We were on the third floor now, still moving ahead. "I don't think it's aliens," I told her.

"Maybe it's jinn? My aunt used to warn me about them and I laughed at her for being so superstitious. Fuck me, maybe she was right?"

"Gin? What, we're all drunk and hallucinating all this? Bollocks?"

"No, jinn, like jinni. Typical Brit, doesn't know a thing about any other religion than his own."

"Brit? What do you consider yourself then?"

"I don't know? Artist, arsehole, lover of artisanal cheeses? I don't fucking know? I don't really put little titles—let alone national identities—on myself like that."

"So just titles on others then?"

"Fucking Brummie."

I'd have laughed if I wasn't terrified. "Since you're in the mood to pontificate, tell me what it was about our first record you liked so much and what we're doing wrong now?"

"Oh god, Codger, you want me to tell you how you lost the plot?"

"Just trying to pass the time as we climb these stairs. Take our minds off of… all this. Forget it."

"It honestly has more to do with my changing than your band changing, though you did go to shit."

"So I have women's lib and punk rock to blame for your defection?"

"No, you have me no longer being a teenager to blame."

"Oh."

"There's nothing wrong with that. The music I make, even though it's for me, chiefly, it's also for teenagers."

"You're saying that kids have changed, our records are no longer relevant to this generation?"

"Well, not your last few. But look at that kid, John, he believed you enough to want to kill you or have you save him or whatever. I don't think there's much a difference in the eyes of fans like that."

"Point?"

"The point is I'm willing to bet his favorite Frivolous Black songs are the early ones, and why? Not just because they're better but because you made them when you were closer to his age and could relate to his experience better than you can now."

"Rock and roll can't grow old can it?"

She looked back. "I don't know. But I suspect if it does it can't expect to keep speaking to the same young people. It has to grow with its audience. If I were in your band you know what I'd do?"

"Sack that Yank singer? I'm miles ahead of you."

"I'd stop trying to sound like you used to and just embrace what you sound like now. Instead of writing for what you think this new generation wants to hear from you, write for the generation that came up with you. That's grown up with you. Better yet, write like you used to, for yourself. Fuck everyone else's expectations." She said it and I could tell this was beyond just me and my mid-life crisis. It was something Rikki herself had needed to hear.

"Sounds like good advice."

"Easier said than done and all that, right?"

I nodded. "Anyways," I said, changing the topic back. "It's not aliens."

"Codger, where are we going?" I wasn't sure if she had heard me. "And if it's not aliens then what is it and where the hell are we? Because this is not Earth."

I wasn't sure how to put it. The things I had experienced in the We led me to different conclusions. "…I think it is Earth, just not our Earth."

This got her to turn around. "What the fuck is that supposed to mean?"

"When We… when I was…" I searched for the right way to put it. Rikki put a hand in front of her mouth and flailed her fingers like a calamari monster. Bingo. I nodded. "I was not only not just myself, I was also not just in that room with you and Marcus."

"Oh, poor fucking Marcus."

Poor fucking Marcus indeed, but I was losing her. "I was in other worlds, all simultaneous."

"Other worlds, exactly. Aliens."

"No, they were other Earths. Some looked exactly like ours. I'm sure there might have been differences had I hung around and picked up a newspaper or a history book but I couldn't do any of those things because I was in torment." She held her hand up and did the calamari again. "Yes, exactly. There were all these parallel universes, right? And there were all these parallel mes. Only some weren't even human, but we were still the same. Somehow we had something in common, we occupied the same space or position in our respective universes or something. And now we occupied the same actual space, we had gotten jammed up, compacted together into that ever-changing mashed-up monster you saw. And the worst part was our thoughts were smashed together too. I was lost in a choir of voices and thoughts, drowned out in some bloody collective hive mind."

She stopped and looked back at me. "That sounds really bad, Codger, I'm sorry."

"It was, it was misery, but..." I wasn't sure if I should even say the next bit, didn't want to give her an excuse to fear me or possibly fry me. "...it was also quite brilliant. It was ecstasy."

"What's this?"

"I was part of an ocean of minds, I wasn't alone. You can't understand because you're like everybody else, you're alone. I was too before I had a glimpse of it. I was alone before and I was burdened by the weight of my own consciousness, but when I was We... when I was with the other mes I was actually free even though I was chained to maybe an endless collection of my parallel selves."

She didn't say anything. Just stared at me like she was considering something important. Then, "Shit, I forgot, I'm out of smokes."

"Rikki, what the fuck? I'm telling you I think we're stuck on a parallel version of Earth and that I experienced a higher form of consciousness and that it was my own somehow and you—"

"I hear you, I really do." She turned around and started walking up the stairs again. "But how is any of that helping us right now? If we're on another Earth, one that's covered in snow and giant tentacle bat things that tear you away up into the sky, what good is knowing that going to do us? Besides, why are we going up? Do you have a plan? I sure as hell don't."

"We're going up because we're looking for that chamber the kid mentioned."

"That kid, the murderer? He was mental, man." But I could hear it in her voice, a little catch. She didn't believe it was a bad plan, not really. "But maybe he wasn't that mental. He said there was a chamber that made music at the top of the hotel, right?"

"He said the whole hotel was one big instrument, built by some mad Darjmainian who was obsessed by the old occult guy Fludd."

"Fludd's the bloke who designed the celestial monochord thing that's on the cover of that old record the *Anthology of American Folk Music*."

I was impressed. "...Right? How did you know?"

"I'm a musician. Just because I don't know how to read sheet music doesn't mean I haven't listened to a lot of stuff. Or done my homework." She turned to give me a smirk. "Besides, my mother thought she was a folky. Loved all that old crackly, recorded into a horn shit. I used to stare at her old LPs for hours while she'd play them and dance arou—"

"That's lovely but shut it for a moment." Before she could tell me to fuck off I held a finger up to stress my seriousness. I could hear something. Something below us, like the creak of a wood floor or a door being shut delicately. Something stirred. But I couldn't decide where it was coming from. I could tell however by the way Rikki was looking at me as well as the fact that she hadn't called me some variation of twat in the last five seconds that she had heard the noise too. I turned around slowly trying to pinpoint the sound. But there was no sound anymore, the trail had stopped dead.

"Do you think someone's down there?" Rikki whispered to me.

"Someone watching us?"

"Maybe? The kid?"

It wasn't a bad theory. "You think we should go down, find out?"

She thought about it. "No, I don't think that he'd be happy to see us, you in particular."

"What happened after I…."

"Imploded like a supernova?"

"Oh, thank Christ, I thought you were going to say super-group."

"You're asking about the kid?"

"He's alive then I take it?"

"Oh, he's alive. After your little laser light show there were just heaps and heaps of bodies, mostly your body, and they were sort of smoldering or glowing in a pile and Marcus said we should get moving in case you, or they I guess, weren't dead."

"The kid?"

"I'm getting to that! So I totally forgot about him, or I guess I assumed he was dead somewhere under that pile of glowing flesh where you used to be. And if Marcus had him on his mind he wasn't telling me about it. So we get the barricade removed finally and then we notice the glow or whatever starting to fade from the pile of flesh or corpses and we decide this is a bad sign and we start grabbing our torches and whatever we're going to need for outside. We're getting ready to run out and that's when the kid comes charging at me, out of fucking nowhere, he knocks me on my ass after running into me with his shoulder. And he's screaming like a banshee the entire time and he just flies past Marcus and goes through the opened door and is gone."

"What the hell?"

"He had one arm, it looked like yo—it had burned it off. Marcus and I tried calling after him, I even ran after him but the kid was a goddamn jackrabbit. When we got to the lobby he was gone."

I looked down the stairwell some more, tried to imagine the kid climbing the stairs slowly waiting for me. Him, with his one good hand wrapped around an axe or maybe even a gun. What if he found a gun, or had it stashed away somewhere? Here I was beset on all sides, contending with otherworldly forces (myself included), weird beasts, witches, angler bat things and even punk rockers and I still had to worry most of all about some fan with a gun. But I didn't hear anything. Couldn't even be sure anymore what I had heard. It sounded like it had come from inside the walls. "Let's get moving. If he's out there then he's out there."

We proceeded, albeit slower than before, more cautiously. "You know what bothers me still?"

"No?" I answered.

"Who was the tall man in the lift with Frankie?"

I had entirely forgot about him. "Hmm, good question. I don't know the answer for certain but after running into the LP witch down in the lobby—"

"Did she come to life again? Me and Marcus almost set her on fire just to make sure she wasn't going to get us. And who killed her? The kid?"

"What? No. No one killed her—that's what I'm getting at— she wasn't even really a corpse, she was a husk. And I suspect

Frankie's mysterious friend on the lift is somewhere in a similar state."

"But why take the form of a giant man in a suit? At least the witch on the flipping album cover makes sense. That's something I know. That's something which has ties to you."

"I dunno, maybe the giant had ties to Frankie?"

"What if it's him who's watching us right now?"

"Why would a giant have to slink around in the shadows, all willy-nilly? He's a fucking giant. He would just come out and get us if that's what he wanted."

Rikki looked somehow wounded that my knowledge of lift giants might eclipse her own. "I don't know what he was or where he is but I don't care to stick around here to prove you wrong or right. Let's get out of here."

We picked up the pace and then that's when we heard it: Something from below us. Whatever it was it was trying to be quiet but it still was making noise. Maybe because it was speeding up as it got closer to us. Rikki's eyes were wide, she could hear it now too. She turned around and we started climbing the stairs in a full-on run. When I started moving faster the cut on my arm started to sting. I wasn't sure if the activity was getting the blood pumping and causing the pain or what but I put a hand over it and pressed down just in case. The thing below us got louder, it must have heard us running now and figured it was no longer time to play it coy. We made it to the fourth floor and my heart was a burning drum in the center of my chest. "Do you have the key to your room on you?" I asked.

"What? Yes, why the shit does it matter? We're only on the fourth floor, my room is up on the twelfth."

But I had seen her on the fourth. I remembered her on the fourth. How? Then it happened. The memory I was trying to put together since I woke up in the pile of my dead selves, another forgotten puzzle piece I had brought back with me, restored to my mind after I clawed out from the We; now it was back. I could see that Rikki was telling the truth, she never had a room on the fourth floor but I did see her on it.

Something below us rounded a corner and collided with a railing there sending a vibration up the staircase to where we were. The vibration was enough to shake my hand off the railing. Maybe the kid had been telling the truth about the way this place was built. It being one giant instrument... Regardless, whatever was down there was big and in quite the hurry to get to us. The fear was useful, it helped me to move even faster and try to catch up to Rikki. She had just turned the corner to the fifth floor and I was about to do the same when I heard it pulsing behind me.

That familiar buzz. The same one I heard all those years ago in Birmingham, England... The Earworm. I had to turn around, had to look at it again. When I did I still couldn't understand fully what I was looking at. A rolling, churning black shape coiled with rows of light which seemed to flicker like street light through half-drawn window shades. There were visual echoes all around it, making it look like a blacklight poster turned into a shell game. It was moving so fast it collided with the left wall and the vibration from that took me and Rikki off our feet. The sound of the collision was massive, like it had smashed into a belfry instead of hotel wall. I dropped my lighter, heard it fall down the stairs. I looked down to watch the dark mass of the creature as it poured up towards me. A fresh hideous bouquet of corruptions blossomed forth from out the rainbow oil slick bramble, metastasizing into billowing, diaphanous limbs. Proving to me yet again that even when utterly terrified I could at least be comforted knowing I'd never have need for a thesaurus. I got to my feet, Rikki screamed something encouraging back towards me, and I rounded the corner and got to the next flight.

This wasn't going to work. The Earworm was too damn fast. And worse, that sound it was making, something about the light that crawled out of the slits that decorated its coils; it called to me. Even stronger than the We, the light called to me. I wanted to turn around, to look into its eyes which weren't eyes at all again. I wasn't going to last much longer. I pounded my feet against the stairs. Past Rikki I could see the door to the sixth floor. There was no way we were going to make it to the seventh. Our lead wouldn't last, the thing was gaining too fast. And that wasn't even putting into account how likely it was that I was going to turn around and just let the big black fucker swallow me up. Then I felt the smallest sliver of that old feeling creep back into me. That feeling of dumb optimism I had waking up from the wreckage in the kitchen. That need to pick up my bass guitar and write something. I didn't care if it was dumb anymore. It was all I had. It was the only part of me that didn't want to surrender to that dark thing coming to pull me under.

We had to change course, there was no other option. The sixth floor was our best bet. "Follow me," Rikki yelled as she pushed open the door to the sixth floor ahead of me. Well, there went my chance to play hero I suppose. I ran after before the door could slam behind her. I took the handle in my hand and closed the door as I entered, hoping it would buy us some time. It did not. Almost the instant I closed the door and started running the Earworm tore right through it like it had been made of paper. The creature filled up the hall with its bent black shape. Up close it resembled some enormous severed black tongue slithering all on its own. The different visual echoes that rippled off it pushed against the debris and the various surfaces of the hall, seeming to prove that all were substantial even if I could see through some of them. I thought of my song, that unborn piece of music that lived inside me and only me, and I turned away from the creature and took off down the hall. I made it around the corner, the buzzing of the Earworm getting close enough to drown out any sort of real thought from my skull. Around the other side of the corner I saw Rikki disappearing into an open door. It wasn't a hotel room, it was a supply closet or something similar. She turned back, scanning for me, and when she caught sight of me she motioned for me to follow her. I had no other choice so I did, hoping that she had enough sense not to dead end us in a supply closet while that thing was sure to see me slip into it.

Luckily the supply closet wasn't a supply closet. Inside there were mops, spray bottles, towels, other supplies including the anus crackers the kid had promised, yes, all of that type of thing, but they only lined the walls. At the center where another wall should have been, instead there was an opening like a tunnel. Rikki disappeared into this and I had no other choice but to follow her into the darkness. I could hear someone ahead of her breathing but I couldn't see their face. It was dark, cold, and wet inside this tunnel and it sounded like I was stepping on stone. Rikki was running up ahead of me, and ahead of her I could see a torch or maybe even a lantern. I followed the light and caught glimpses of the walls as we got further and further in. The walls were indeed stone, black bricks irregularly patterned and dripping with moisture. I looked behind me quickly to see if the Earworm followed, then realized if it did, how was I going to see it? The blasted thing was as black as the walls here. I could only see the light that threatened to escape from its fissures when I was close up to the thing and it was in motion. And that wasn't a position I was looking forward to returning to. So I kept my head turned around the right way and followed the flame which led us onward, and upward too, I noticed. Below me the stones made a gradual staircase.

After another few moments I understood that the tunnel we had been in had given way to a spiral staircase that was taking us up. I knew where we were going and I knew who was leading us there. "John." I whispered it but the word broke the quiet like thunder. The fire stopped hovering ahead and it froze for a moment... then started floating back toward me. The kid appeared with it a few seconds later. With his remaining hand he held a lantern colored gold and shaped like an upside down owl. The arm he lost, that I... that We had taken appeared to have been cauterized by the bite just below the elbow. Even though it was neat and clean looking it made me sick to see what I had done. Next to him was Rikki. I could see she had her knife out, she was no fool. The kid looked at me like he wanted to tear my head off but knew it'd cost him too much. That reminded me of Sully, actually. I told him, "I know where you're taking us, can it help get us back home?"

"So you know where we are now," the kid said. "Us getting home? That would depend on you." He raised his smooth-skinned stump up and I winced. "I can't exactly play music anymore, can I, dude?"

"So you think I can play whatever instrument is in this bloody music chamber at the top of this secret staircase and that it'll take us back to where we come from?"

"If someone else answers a question with another question I'm going to stab them in the ear, got it?" Rikki said.

We went silent. Then...

"...Did she?"

"Probably, but who knows?"

"Yeah, it might take us back if you play it right."

"'Might'? Fucking hell." I looked at the kid's face, tried to imagine such a young face killing someone else. That was just my privileged, rich English ass not realizing how easy it was to kill when you believed in some gobshite barmy shit that told you it was okay. That it was necessary even. Vietnam, my generation's biggest lesson and biggest blunder, always coming back into the conversation. "Before I ask you how this is supposed to work, what makes you so sure I'm the one who knows the song to begin with?"

The kid actually smiled. "It's gotta be you. It's all based on your band's music. The Master, the Unquiet One, wants you. He chose you in Birmingham and now he's after you again to collect what's his."

I was happy to finally know more than anyone else. "Master, huh? Sorry, but it doesn't want me." The kid's head tilted. Then I spelled it out to him. "It wants her."

Visitation Rites

Rikki had been in my room on the fourth floor. And she wasn't alone. I'm not just talking about me; sure, I was there but I wasn't much company. Rikki and her chaperon had been there the night before all this started happening, before I woke up in the closet feeling like death warmed over's uglier cousin. I was two days into kicking the coke and the bottle and I thought that's why I was getting on so miserably. It felt like my insides were shredding themselves and the blood in my veins was thick tar. Sure, it had been worse than the other time I tried to kick but I was getting older, I assumed I was just in a weaker state. John Lennon's death had brought me to a critical depression and that was probably enabled by my guilt and anger at Sully for making us have to kick him out of the group. But none of that was what was wrong with me. All of it was true but what was really rotting me inside out was something left inside me a long time before, and it wanted out.

I could remember it all now. I was on my bed, fever sick, foaming at the mouth, twisted into a ball wearing only my bathrobe. Typical junkie. Typical ungrateful rock star feeling sorry for himself. Disgraceful, really. I had two bowls left from housekeeping for me, one on the floor next to the bed and one on the nightstand in case I couldn't make it to the floor, and I still managed to miss them both and get sick all over the sheets. Somehow the toes of one of my feet were covered in a thick coat of vomit, and then I remembered I had stepped in the floor bowl at some point. But there I was, certain I was dying and for once I wasn't just being dramatic; I actually was dying. Marcus had said this whole process usually killed whoever it happened to. Usually. Me and Keith Richards, who'd have thought it? My body was shutting down, my mind was on fire. Then I saw the door open and I became calm. It was here. And it brought a friend.

Rikki Fucking Spectre waltzed into my room, her pupils swollen to blank black dots. She was in its thrall. Behind her poured in the Earworm, in the guise of a more gentlemanly shape. The same shape I remember back in Birmingham. Its eyes, the burning windows, fixed to its skull or helm. The door shut behind it and I laid back on my bed, fingers digging into the vomit- and piss-soaked sheets like they were my mother's arms. I was a frightened child and Rikki was what looked terrifying, more a witch then than in any of her cheap publicity shots. She knelt down before me, the Earworm behind her shifted its black form like a cloak and then produced a long shining and skinny forearm with an open hand on its end. It was her master and she was its pet and now it wanted to give her her treat. In that moment I realized I was more than its pet, I was its slave. And then the worst pain I had yet experienced took me over. I could feel something inside me burning its way out, trying to return to its master. I felt like I was being impaled or hung on horns. I had the peculiar image of a black tree that had grown inside me but was now upside down, uprooted, torn out of its hold from my insides and taking chunks of me with it. Something was now in my throat, making its way to the air. I was hunched over like a pleading monk and I was face to face with Rikki. If she was in there at all she had a hell of a poker face. Over her head hung the hand of the Ear-worm waiting patiently. And to its beckon, finally, the burning gift it had given me so long ago came rushing back to return to its grasp.

Once it was outside of me it looked so small; it was a lot like having a rotten tooth that felt like it was the size of a small castle in your gums, but when the dentist pulled it out you're embarrassed to find it such a tiny thing that had caused you all that distress. In the Earworm's palm was a black seed. Instantly I could feel a void it had left inside me where it once resided. I could also feel my fever flood back over me. I collapsed backward onto the bed. I didn't know what was happening to me yet, I was still under the sway of the Earworm too, but I could feel something changing in me. The seed, whatever it was, whatever talents it had given me, it was not only a key but a lock. It granted me access to wherever ideas come from but it also kept that place from opening me up. That was gone now. And instead I had an unguarded small entrance within that already felt like it was growing bigger. Before I passed out I could see the Earworm looming over Rikki, revealing her navel and inserting the seed into her like it had done to me ten years prior.

So this is what I told Rikki and the kid as we continued walking the stone steps hidden inside the walls of the Alucinari Hotel. For Rikki it was a lot to take in.

Altered Hymns

"… I thought it was a dream." She still had her knife hanging by her side. With her other hand I thought I saw her feeling at her belly like an expectant mom-to-be but it was dark and hard to tell. I was still nervous not being able to tell if the Earworm was lurking behind us, climbing the darkened path with us. "I mean, I didn't really remember much of it… just being led around by some black shape with the burning holes in its face where eyes should be. I remembered you on a bed but I… I don't know. To be honest, I had been thinking of you."

"Really?" I was surprised.

"Yeah, I knew Frivolous Black was in the hotel too, and I was thinking about that first LP and how much I loved it when I was younger. That first fucking song, the title track, how fucking scary it was. I just assumed the black shape in my dream was me thinking about that song. And you being on the bed writhing around looking like a corpse was all on account of me being nervous to meet you and sort of sad about what… became of you."

I was bleeding, on the run for my life and soul in a parallel version of Earth that was stuffed with monsters that were only slightly less frightening than the monster I myself had become a mere few hours before being led to what almost certainly was a dead end or trap by a murderous Yank who probably had it in for me on account of me munching off his arm in my afore-mentioned monstrous state, and what was I concerned with? Somebody young and cool confirming my suspicion that I was a has-been. Had my priorities straight, didn't I? "'Became of me'? It's okay to say it, Rikki. I'm irrelevant. A fuck up. Worse, a cliché. I know."

"No," she started to say. "...Yeah, all that. But who isn't? Chances are, when it comes my time I'll be one too. You were right before, I am afraid of making a new record. Because what if it isn't as good? Or what if I want to do something different and nobody gives it a chance because they want me to be ex-actly like I was before? Nobody wants something they love to change. But it has to, right? Even if you try and maintain what you were, eventually you just become a distorted imitation of what you used to be, or worse, what you think people want of you... So you're fucked." She laughed. "Either way, no one gets to ride the high horse the whole time, right? And besides, you were flipping brilliant in your day, man. You and Frivolous put out more good shit on one album than any songwriter would be happy to put out in one career; which means yeah, to look at you now, yes, you're a tremendous fuck up. And... that's commendable if being a fuck up is inevitable."

"I think... I think that actually makes me feel better." It did. "Okay, I've given up my secret, tell us yours, kid."

He walked ahead a bit of a distance. He only had one arm and it was holding a lantern, but I still felt nervous around him. "You wanna know what that seed is that the Master has given you?"

"You still think this thing is your master, then?" I asked him.

He thought about it. "...Not really. I just don't know what else to call him. Sounds cooler than fucking Earworm anyway." I shook my head even though he wasn't looking at me. "Right now what we're walking towards is a church."

"A bleeding church in the middle of a hotel," Rikki said. "Of course, it's already got a secret staircase in the middle that looks like a castle's asshole." She wasn't wrong.

"This is the church I belong to. We lost ownership of the hotel before I was born so we had to break in here, to get to Frivolous Black and Frankie Gideon. We weren't sure which of you had the seed. We didn't think it was both."

"What's the seed I have in my fucking belly button?" Rikki asked.

"Oh yeah, sorry. The seed, as far as my church can tell, is what the—"

"Earworm," I said.

"...Thing uses to grant whomever it finds worthy the ability to hear its song."

"What is its song?" Rikki asked.

"I touched it," I said. "Or I suppose it touched me. And then later when I got lost in all those other versions of myself, what I saw sort of made sense of what it showed me. The Earworm is some sort of entity that exists in a possibly endless amount of parallel universes simultaneously. And doing this has made it sort of like a god and sort of completely fucking mental at the same time. Because it was never meant to be a god. At least that's what was happening to me when I became lost. And the music, this music it can hear, is the only thing that can make sense of its existence. It needs this music because it's not just music."

The kid stopped walking. "It's never just music." I could hear his sneakers as they turned around. "There's a reason why music is the most powerful of all the arts. There's a reason why they banned the playing of the augmented fourth in the middle ages. There's a reason why even animals can be lulled by a song. Music is magic. Lyrics can be incantations or spells. This world we walk upon is but one of countless others just like it. Each bounded together by a shared vibration that keeps them in place. This vibration is this particular universe. Vibration is music, music is vibration. Every single being has a unique vibration. You, me, her, and everything else. The rocks we're walking on, this lantern in my hand… My church has known this for centuries. But even though everything in this hotel, us three included, are bound together by a shared vibration that means we belong to this universe, we also each have a special vibration that's unique to just us. And we're the only ones, the only things in our universe who can have it. But there are other universes, as you know, and there are other beings, other things there that share your special vibration. These are your shadow selves."

"Doesn't sound so special to me then," I said.

"Shut up, Codger. I actually think I'm following this, go on," Rikki said.

"And what the seed does is allow you to access these other selves you have across the web of universes. Anything that shares your vibration. You view it as inspiration or daydreaming or a sudden change in temperament or mood, but it's really you gleaning from these reflections of yourselves. And what you all possess is an ability to hear the music the… Earworm craves. So now with this seed that ability has been amplified."

"We already had the talent, then?" I said. "Earworm just gave us a Marshall stack?"

"Exactly. All the beings that share your vibration, you all have the talent so you feed each other and through you, the seedbearer—"

"Oooh, don't like that," Rikki said.

"...All this is channeled through and you can make the music it wants."

"What does it want it for?" Rikki said. "Will it fix it, make it normal, no longer all fractured up into a thousand million other dimensions or whatever?"

"We... we actually don't know." The kid said it and I gave a laugh. He started walking again. I think he might have been upset. "What? We don't know for certain anything."

"So you've worshipped this thing, built a hotel which is actually a giant monochord or some such yampy nonsense just to summon it or whatever, hell, you've even killed for it, and you don't know what it wants? You don't know if it even wants you or your help."

"We know this," the kid started. "Something went wrong a long time ago. Someone built something just like this church and the music chamber inside this hotel and tried to play along with the vibration of the universe or alter it somehow, transpose it in some way, and they made a mistake. Or worse, they did it on purpose... but doing this created the Master or the Earworm or whatever it is. Trapped it in that state it's in. But it also might be the reason why everyone, everywhere, whatever religion they have or don't, whatever color their skin is, or language they speak, everyone agrees that something's wrong with the world. It's the only universal truth. Something is fucked up with the world, with us. And maybe that's because something really is wrong. Whatever made this thing fucked everything else up too."

"Knocked us off our axis, changed the pitch of our vibration, made a dissonance where there was once harmony?" I said.

"Dude, exactly."

"Lovely thought, really," I told him. "But I don't think so. Even though there's monsters and inter-dimensional fallen god demon type things, it doesn't change the fact that the reason the world is fucked up is because there are a lot of shitty people doing shitty things, and half the time they're not even trying to do shitty things, they're just too fucking stupid to know that what they're doing is shitty." The kid didn't have anything to say to that.

We kept going up. I didn't hear the Earworm behind us. Didn't even feel that it was following us. Like it wanted us to get to the chamber. And that was even worse than being chased by it.

"What do you think the monster wants?" Rikki asked me.

I thought about it: That relentless hunger for the sound it chased that I had felt when our minds were joined. And then my own impulses when I was made like it, compacted and fractured. "I think it just wants to share its suffering. Purest form of the blues, really."

"It wants the world to be like it, in chaos?" Rikki asked.

"Worlds," the kid corrected.

"Maybe," I said. "It's hell but it's heaven too."

"It's definitely a possibility," the kid said.

"And you're okay with that?" I asked.

We climbed higher, the kid kept talking. "I don't know what I'm okay with anymore. I was raised in the church, so was my mother and my father, it's all I've ever known. But seeing the Unquiet One close up, seeing what happens to the seedbearers after the gift has been removed and they're left to shuffle in and out of all their other selves... if that's what's in store for us all... I don't know. Maybe we were wrong this whole time. I don't know, but Codger seems to think it wasn't all bad, so then again...?"

"Why did it bring us here? Why drop the whole hotel here in this version of the world? Is this where it's from?" I was tired of philosophy, I wanted to know what to actually do, not why we were doing it.

"It didn't bring us here, I did," the kid said. "It was an accident. Our mission was simple: Frivolous Black was going to be staying in the Alucinari. Even though we, the church, no longer controlled the hotel, we paid attention to it, we had certain ears to the ground. When we knew you'd be here we thought it would be the perfect time to try and get a seedbearer to operate the music chamber. But the thing is, we didn't know if all three of you—"

"Four, four in the band," Rikki said.

"No, that little American imp doesn't count," I countered.

"Yeah, there's no way that guy's a seedbearer," the kid agreed.

"I happen to like his voice, it's operatic," Rikki said. "He's got more range than Sullivan anyway."

"The thing is, or was, we didn't know if all the original members of the band had been given seeds or not. The church has been studying this for centuries and we know that sometimes when there's a group not everyone gets a seed. Sometimes it's just the songwriter or whoever shapes the music the most. Other times it's more than one member or the entire band. Those are usually the most powerful artists, their work can be revolutionary, it can create whole new forms of sound and music."

"Why doesn't the Earwig or whatever just give everyone a seed so they can change music each time and get closer to this sound it's after so badly?" Rikki asked.

"We think that it only has a small number of these seeds. That's why it comes to collect them if an artist…"

"Goes to shit," I finished for him.

"Deviates too far from the sound it wants. If you stop being useful to it, it comes back and takes what it gave you so it can reinvest it somewhere else, give them a shot."

"Fickle fucking monster, isn't it?" I said.

"Back to why and how you brought us to this shitty place?" Rikki said.

"Sorry, I think I'm still a little high," the kid said. "I toked up after I got away from Codger and was tripping the fuck out about my arm." This fucking kid. "And it's just a theory but whatever thing you were when you took my arm, Codger… do you know if you or it had some sort of venom or something?"

"Sorry, I've no idea. Why, do you feel sick?"

"No, actually the opposite. I felt this insane rush of energy after the pain wore off. It's fucking weird… like whatever got into my system was a paralytic but since it's from another dimension it's all fucked up and wasn't prepared for someone like me so now I'm kinda stoned."

"Or maybe you're just stoned because you got stoned," Rikki said. "Why are we here?"

"We're here because I was messing around in the chamber, I've done it in the past a few times with no problems, but I played some sequence of music this time and then all of a sudden there was crazy fucking pressure on me. Like I was stuck to the wall in a Gravitron or whatever at the fair. And then I just passed out. I woke up and everything was dark. I left the chamber, went to a window, and at first I thought everything was normal. This was after the hotel had been evacuated from the storm, so I figured that's why the power was out. But I kept looking out into the snow and then I saw one of those things, those big towers, it wasn't a building, it was something else. And I saw the lights, those animals next."

"So why didn't you go back and play the song again?" I said. "Do you actually want to be here?"

"I did go back and I did play it again, back when I could still play anything… But nothing happened. I don't know if that's because I wasn't playing the exact same thing the exact same way or if it didn't matter because I was just playing the song that matched up to this universe, where we're at now, not the song that matched up to our original universe. This has never happened before. Everyone in the church talks about all this shit, but it's all just theories and superstitions like any other church I guess. But this actually fucking worked and I don't have a clue why."

"So the hotel is some sort of spaceship that can travel through dimensions if you play the right song in it?" Rikki sounded exhausted.

"Sort of," the kid told her.

"What made you think I could play the song that'd get us home?" I asked.

"Or send us into some sort of multidimensional hell place, you know, whichever?" Rikki said.

Finally we came to the top of the stone steps. The kid held up his lantern and I could see a massive round wooden door. "I need help with the door." The kid waved his stump in my direction.

I walked over to the door to pull but not before telling Rikki, "Watch him." The kid backed up in response, giving me space as I pulled on the door handle and dragged the door open. I watched from the corner of my eye, making sure the kid didn't come darting over.

He couldn't hold a knife without dropping the lantern but who's to say he wouldn't just bash me with the lantern and be done with it? But he didn't move. And Rikki watched him like a cat. As I finished moving the heavy wooden door I noticed her rubbing her belly again. This time I knew I saw it.

We came into the chamber and it actually felt like a church to me. Like the one I used to go to with my mom when I was still a lad. Solemn, deadly serious, calming. The chamber seemed immense, built from the same stone as the steps. And it was round. The kid went around with his lantern lighting torches located along the sides. With the light I could see that at the center of the room there laid what looked like a throne made from pipe that reached into the ceiling. It was some sort of organ, only it looked like its parents were Battersea Power Station and a bagpipe that had a little bit of spider in it from its mother's side. "The door," Rikki said and we started moving it back together. Then we walked over to the organ where the kid was standing.

He put his lantern down to rest on the bench that sat next to the coiled pile of the thing. His hand rested on what looked like the keyboard but upon closer inspection I saw a collection of keys and strings. I looked down towards the lantern and saw foot pedals feeding into the thing on the ground too. "How the fuck do you expect me to play this thing?" I said. "I play bass because I'm not good enough to play guitar in a band where the guitar player keeps it simple because he cut off the tips of his fingers in an industrial accident. What the fuck am I supposed to do with this mess?"

With his one good hand the kid pulled a string then tapped out a beat on one of the crooked black keys. The sound that came out of the thing was low, scuttling and sharp beneath the bass blast. I had never heard anything quite like it. Not sure if that was a good thing. Like most church music it had a distinct lack of balls. But then again, it was all church music then, wasn't it? Mine included. "It sounds better when I have two hands to play it."

"Who told you to reach out and try to touch me when I was a fucking hydra?"

I put my fingers on one of the keys, pressed down, and the

spider made a hiss from one of its legs. The hiss wasn't especially melodious. "So since I have the fucking seed inside me now should I be the one to play us home?" Rikki asked. She took a finger to one of the strings and plucked. It sounded worse than my hiss.

"This was your fucking plan then," I started. "Us fingering away blindly at this thing like it's an eighth grade date at the movies?"

"Fuck you, dude. I don't know, I thought one of you would know what to do," the kid said. "I'm just a fucking kid, you're adults... adults are supposed to know what to do. My parents and their stupid fucking church told me to kill that guy so I did it because they were in charge. And now I'm finding out it's all bullshit. And you, you're all bullshit too. You don't even appreciate how lucky you are. You pretend to but you don't. I thought you were a genius but you don't know shit. Just like me and all the rest of the fuck ups." His eyes were wet. "I'm doing the best I can, man." He shoved me with his one arm. I backed up a little before finding my footing, then I took him by the wrist and stopped him from doing anything more. He tried to wrestle free but I had him. I wanted to be mad at him, he was a murderer, a fuck up beyond even my expertise, but I couldn't. He was just a broken puppet realizing its own strings only now after they'd been severed. Young, dumb, but not evil, just bred and raised to carry it out. He was right, we were adults, he was just a kid. He was an errand boy like the rest of us.

"I'm sorry, John." He wouldn't stop trying to get at me. "Hey, John, I'm sorry. None of us know what to do and we should." He stopped fighting with me and I let go of his hand. "What you played before, was it something we know, can you tell us how to play it?"

He smiled like a dope. "Yeah, I think so. It was bits and pieces of different Friv songs, but sort of pulled together like one big medley. Then I kind of did my own thing. It all started with the title track, the augmented f—" There was that familiar buzz, only since we were in the chamber the sound was amplified into a clockwork moan. The stucco of the black bricks started glowing the same red glow that the lift had back with Frankie in the lobby. The same color as the slits in the Earworm's coils. I could hear something under the floor moving, something large and mechanical, like a factory. I used to work in a factory with Vinnie before the band took off. I knew that sound. It was the one I was running from by joining a band and trying to do something other than what my dad had done for a living... The industrial sound kept grinding and then the floor shifted. The black bricks underneath us moved up and some moved down. The walls were burning with the glow of the Earworm. All of them scrolling down or rapidly shifting themselves to the side, a poltergeist in control of a demonic abacus made from coal. It felt like whatever was happening was now happening faster and then the organ, the great pipe spider in the center of the room, started twisting its way around. The pipes burst as it was snapped from the ceiling. The broken remains became coated with the red light from the wall, turning and twisting down into the floor then swallowed up by it. From the remaining organ pipes on the ceiling dripped a thick black liquid, some of which spilled onto my forehead. There went that plan. I wiped off whatever had fallen from the pipe. The door into the chamber smashed to pieces but instead of the Earworm waiting behind it was only black. Nothing. I watched the walls move some more and it hit me: we were going up.

The remaining pipes of the organ that stuck out like stalactites reared up into the ceiling as the black bricks above us revolved clockwise. The red line that framed each brick grew in intensity as the pieces began to fall away from the roof just as the floor stopped shifting and we came to a rest. As more and more of the ceiling disappeared I saw flecks of white in the air: snow, and behind that, stars… or maybe just those terrible lights… the anglers. The remains of the organ still rested in the middle of the room but was now bathed in the red light. It looked like it had been dipped in lava when it started to become something else entirely. The last bricks fell away from the room and I saw that we were outside now, on top of the building. The snow fell down delicately, almost a mercy. I looked out at Rikki and saw her staring up at the night sky. Above us storm clouds rolled in like some Old Testament Hollywood movie starring Charlton Heston. The buzzing had stopped and my head felt clear, the snow and the cold almost soothing.

"Codger, look." The kid's voice startled me, I turned over to him. He was standing near the center of the roof, next to the red glowing pile that had been the organ. He wasn't alone.

Standing in front of him were three figures. Vinnie Izzloni, Burt Dank, and Sully Sullivan. Frivolous Black. Impossible. What was this that stood before me?

Friv Today, Die Tomorrow

They looked just like I remembered them. Not the last time I saw them, but the last time I was happy to see them. Six years ago, give or take. Right after we recorded our third record, *Summoner of Sorrows*, before we started taking a bump every time our elbows slipped on the record button, back when we still were just smoking a shit ton of weed. Back when we still had something to say musically that felt fresh. Back when we were friends. That was the Frivolous Black that stood before me. All three of them stared back with an empty sort of recognition, like how a deer or a rabbit will stare at you when they know you're watching. Were they human? Or just another imitation like the LP witch or whoever the giant man who led Frankie on to the elevator had been? Did they look younger, really look younger, or had they survived the extraction of their own seeds like me? Did they make it through the descent into their fractured other selves and emerge stronger, healthier than they'd felt in years after they clawed their way out of a heap of husks that shared their own face?

I pushed past the kid and got right up in front of them. Sully walked towards me, lifting his chin up slowly, the way he always did when he started to talk. But he didn't say anything. He didn't have to. It felt like a knot had gotten itself loose in my head, like concentric rings on a pond suddenly smoothing themselves to a calm. Then Sully's mind and mine were at one. I could feel him with me, not controlling me but open to me. And then the others stood by him and the cord inside my head became even looser. All four of us had been joined. It wasn't quite like before when I had been part of the We or even when the Earworm had sent its transmission to me. This was different. I didn't have access to any vital personal information or emotion, every single one of us simply had one impulse, one singular desire: we wanted to play. This desire was so compulsive that I barely registered that sickening buzzing sound returning and I paid little notice to Rikki screaming out a warning to me and the kid.

It looked like the night had come alive and taken him. His small frame was a sugar cube dropped into a cup of coffee, disturbing its dark contents before being swallowed whole by them. The Earworm had emerged from the night air itself and the kid fell away screaming into its black swirling mass. I could make out his last words, "…not my master, I don't follow—" but then his words gave way to screams. I could see the kid's eyes locked on to my own, see how the skin on his skull was stripped away layer by layer, revealing a mask of muscle and blood until this too was stripped and the brilliant white of bone shimmered out bright as any other star in the sky. I could see his eyes still pleading to me, his hero, to save him; I could see all of this and I could not have cared less. Even when the kid's eyes and their nest of bone receded into wherever the Earworm would now keep them. I could only register that these things had occurred, I had no feelings otherwise. So I turned away from the flowing witch hair tangle of the beast's body and the red light there screaming out from within its coils. I was wholly uninterested and neither was my band; they followed me as I went towards the center of the tower we now stood on.

The entire surface of the tower was now washed in the strange red light. It had deposited itself into an intricate grid of sorts and we passed through it unharmed until we got to where all the red light seemed to flow like blood rivers back to the sea. The shattered remains of the music chamber's organ, bathed in the red, were reconstructing themselves, swelling and expanding as if given breath, and then they became taller than us all. This red mass that looked volcanic or like molten steel oozed up, somehow becoming solid, and we were dwarfed by it. We waited. Moving and resting as one like a pack of dogs. It cooled down, or the light dissipated, and still we waited. We knew what was going to happen. What we needed to happen.

The red light crept away and in the place where the organ once sat instead there was a high black wall that curled over at the top, making it look like a black wave at its highest before it broke. From the center of this curled tip hung a large black bell. In front of this sat Burt's drum set, just the way he always laid it out. Our old logo, the wavy one, stretched across his bass drum head. Surrounding the kit were four small pillars that looked made of polished onyx or some dark gemstone. On each pillar sat an item. To the left, Vinnie's guitar, to the right, Sully's microphone, and right before me was my bass. My old Ibanez, the purple one that I had used to record most of our first three records. The one that Sully had smashed to pieces when I had made the mistake of using it on stage one night in Cleveland and he had a right cob on. That bass had a bit of my old girlfriend's nail polish on the back of it, it was her initials and the date at the time... April 7th, 1973. I didn't have to check, I knew the guitar I held in my hands now would have the same marking. Just like we didn't need to check to know that none of these instruments were plugged in and that it wouldn't matter at all. They wouldn't need electricity to sound or to become amplified. Whatever the Earworm used to power lifts, that red light, it was more than enough to let us be heard now.

Part of me, the part that was still solely me, distantly observed the Earworm scuttling past Rikki then taking to the air, leaving long trails of colors behind it. Lightning flashed overhead revealing a sky filled with a frenzy of those wriggling monstrosities with the lights. Swimming through the air, the anglers circled the tower like sharks. The Earworm flashed red, green, blue, yellow as it arced through the air dispersing some of the beasts with the lights before the remaining creatures started to orbit it like satellites. The worm swelled in mass and still the creatures circled it cautiously. They couldn't help themselves, all of them in the black star's sway. Below this Rikki stood across from the band, her eyes wholly black now, like back in the hotel room when she took the seed that was once mine. Why wasn't the Earworm using her now for its song? She still had her seed, I didn't. Why me, why us now? Was it just giving us a proper send-off before it tore us apart? Or perhaps we, or I had changed now that I'd come back from the brink? Maybe it thought I was useful again. Maybe it thought I knew its song better than the punk rocker again. The dark globes that were Rikki's eyes seemed to flash at me. She waited, like every other terror in this world, for us to begin. It was time. I took a long breath, held it in my lungs like I was diving. The change was complete. I stopped looking at Rikki, I stopped being an I and became We again. Only now We were Frivolous Black and We served one purpose. Thunder overheard. Thunder and then some more lightning. Finally the rain started to fall. Not snow anymore, rain. That same rain that had always been falling.

The bell entered. Once, twice. Thunder. Three times, four

times, five times… thunder. Six, seven, eight…

We came in with a sound like a waking behemoth. Vinnie's guitar was pure menace, the tritone positively sinister, my bass underneath it muscular and fuzzy. Burt splashed on the cymbals, rolled on the toms. Our sound was a deep, dark swamp, you could drown in us if you fell in or jumped. The only thing that could cut through this exquisite sludge was Vinnie's guitar, a gnarled black tree reaching out from the water with bent crooked fingers. We were Frivolous Black, this was "Frivolous Black," and this was what We were meant to do. This sound was the reason why We four were born, why We came together, why We will be remembered. This was why the Earworm was drawn to us, to me. But there was no me, there was only We. We didn't have to think, didn't have to worry about getting out of pocket, about Vinnie speeding up after his solos, throwing the tempo to shit, We didn't have to worry about Sully forgetting the fucking words to a song of our own that We've played hundreds of times before. Words that only he could sing. Words that I wrote.

Now We'd cooled, Burt just gently moved on the toms as Vinnie's guitar hit that devil's chord, again and again. Everything We did now was to build anticipation for Sully's entrance. For the spell We've been casting all these years to truly become complete. This sound is what gives our lives meaning. It could never be made by anyone but us four. Us four at that exact time in our lives. We sounded good. Better than good, We sounded like a fire in the heart of the sun. Sully put the mic to his lips. But We didn't sound like We did when We recorded this song. Because We were not those men. Not anymore or maybe at all.

With a grace I had never before known I lifted up my bass in my hands, held it over my head, letting the guitar strap slip off my right shoulder, and then took the neck of the instrument in my hands like it was the hilt of a sword and sent the body of this perfect copy of my Ibanez bass directly into Sully Sullivan's ever-angelic-looking face. It hit so hard the tremor it sent up my arms hurt my teeth. It hit so hard I could see the bass embedded in Sully's face, like a bowling ball thrown into a TV set. Pieces of bone fragment or maybe something else caking the sides of the wound spilled out like confetti. But before I could investigate further, find out whether or not I'd just killed my old friend or merely something made to look like him, I pulled out the bass with a loud wet THUNK and Sully stumbled backward and then fell off the tower. I rushed to the side, thinking idiotically I could reach down and save him. Even though it had been me who sent him on his fucking way. I peered over and thanks to the lightning could see Sully or this imitation of him falling into what must have been thousands of nightmares gathered together on the ground. None of them looked human, even from this great height. Some had eyes which glinted yellow like wolves as they looked up the tower at me. Others didn't even seem to have eyes at all, nor faces. A crepuscular coalition of things that usually only live below. Below in the pits of the ocean or below the surface of the earth itself, these were things that didn't belong crawling along on the land. Maybe they weren't even indigenous to this place, maybe these were just factions of the Earworm itself, maybe it had dissected itself, made itself legion in order to give us a fitting audience for the wretched song we were to play for it.

The Earworm hung in the heavens above, bigger now than the moon in the sky.

Rain seemed to fall away from it, its halo of swarming beasts moving rapidly around almost as if to translate its fury or disappointment with me. Those burning windows it had instead of eyes grew wide and seemed to burn straight into me even from this distance. I shouted up at it, "I don't do requests, I'm not a fucking jukebox." And then it started coming down towards me. The red light burning all around it and through it. I turned my head, wanting to run but knowing there was nowhere to go; I was stuck at the top.

"...Hey, can we give it a shot?" Rikki was there holding Sully's glowing red mic in her hand. Her eyes were no longer black, at least any blacker than usual. She still had that raccoon makeup piled around them on account of the rain and the girl's own poor taste. "Come on, you old burnt out Brummie."

"Flash in the pan."

"Fossil."

I nodded and then I didn't have to anymore. Rikki was with me and I was with her, joined mentally. I could sense the seed she still carried inside her. The long black branches growing from it, filling up the spaces within her. And the others too, Vinnie and Burt, or whatever they actually were, they were with us as well, only now they or the Earworm weren't in control of me or Rikki. We had the majority share, with the seed we had the control. I slung my bass back on and started walking on the E string with my fingers. I didn't have to look behind me to see that the Earworm had stopped its descent, this I could see through Rikki's eyes. The black stain in the sky hovering just above the tower just behind me had stopped and was waiting. It wanted to know what we were going to play next. So did I.

I remembered the song I had wanted to play, to write after first waking up among the husks of all the other Codgers. After surfacing from the weight of infinite possibilities... The song, the song that only I could hear. I quieted everything else in the world and followed only its voice. Let it lead me where it wanted. How it wanted. I played along to its suggestions, trying to… not recreate it… but just help it to be born. To carry it through, from dream into real. And then it was time for the others to join in. I was grateful, I was never much for bass solos. Any solo that overstayed its welcome, actually. We were in tune, perfectly moving as one organism, and we came crashing in with one sudden gallop. This wasn't Frivolous Black, this was something altogether new.

Rikki's voice careened through our electric murk, I'd never heard her sound like this. She was fiercer than before, but then the rest of us were playing more elegantly than we ever had too. Elegant, but not delicate. Our sound was still us, still dark, passionate, solid as stone, but we had turned a new corner which suited us. And it may have suited the Earworm too. It started to spiral itself, around and around. The barnacles surrounding it seemed afraid of this new behavior and they swam away erratically. They collided with one another as our music built momentum. I walked to the edge of the tower, looked down into the hordes of devils waiting below. I saw some of them climbing the tower with their stalks and claws, yellow eyes sparkling up. The swarm on the ground below moved with our music, along with it, against it. I could see their violence to one another, it appeared rhythmic. The music compelled them to tear one another apart, to war, to dance. It was all the same. And we kept playing. This new song, this new sound, we let it guide us as we guided it. It was all the same. Rikki sang words which were her own and also mine. Vinnie and Burt became mere instruments that we played. Or maybe that's all Rikki and I were to them. How was I to know? All I knew was that there was no need for explanation or communication, this was pure expression. We could write as we played and never hit a wrong note. As long as we followed that voice which more and more seemed to be our own, echoing back across the dark of our minds.

There was a great crunch above and the sky started to split apart. Massive cracks of red light, like the Earworm had made before, fissured directly into the night in some increasingly complex pattern that continued to grow. The ground shook; I could see some of the slithering beasts scaling the tower fall off to the chaos below. Others continued to climb.

The red cracks in the night started spreading, each appearing with a low horrible sound, like water swirling down the drain rapidly until it became an ugly croak. If this was the Earworm's doing I couldn't say, for its part it continued to undulate, spinning and spasming either in great pain or tremendous ecstasy. Knowing what I did of its state of existence I'd wager it was a good amount of both. Not that I cared, I just kept playing. I kicked my foot off the edge of the tower and turned back to Rikki. She was a manic shadow brought to life, swinging her hair back and forth in gorgon frenzy while she purred and roared into the microphone. Stretching words neither of us had thought of before to sound like something we'd never known but had always felt. Our eyes met for the briefest of moments, and we knew we'd never have to say another word to one another again. It wouldn't be necessary. It would only be a let-down. Words could never compete with this form of communication. We were closer now than two people were ever meant to be. Deeper than friendship, family, or lovers; deeper still than what I felt when I was lost in the We. Because this was beyond just me.

Beyond her. We had become a new galaxy unto ourselves. I thought of the kid, or maybe it was Rikki thinking it. We thought of the way he died and what he had said, tried to say. *He lived the way he died.* Metal... The ground shook some more and it sounded like the tower was crumbling. Above us the Earworm was buzzing again, maybe singing along, maybe screaming for us to stop. I couldn't care less about that or where we were all going. I just wanted to keep playing. Only wanted to find out where the song would take us next. Not whether or not it took us back home, or to some state of perpetual suffering that mirrored the Earworm's purgatory. That was of little consequence to me. What I wanted to know was where we could take the music next. That was it.

Something with yellow burning eyes had made its way onto the top of the tower with us but of course I wasn't concerned. It seemed to be moving unnaturally slow. Lurching this way at a comical crawl. Everything was moving slowly now. Time had become a syrup, you could get through it but it took work to wade your way through. Above, things started sinking up into the sky. Pieces of the tower, various forms of life, those blasted angler creatures. All slipping up into the red haze of the light which had gone from a series of intricate cracks to a burning surface suspended above us. All of this was affected by the new slow drip of time. Only the frenzy of the Earworm itself seemed to be free of these effects. It may have even been moving faster. While this was interesting, I wasn't, for the first time in a long time, overly concerned with time and its passing. The past, the future, I'd left them both behind, and when they fell away they fell away like scales from my eyes. The present was the only thing I could see.

That's where I am right now. That moment at the end when the song usually fades, you know, right when it's starting to get good. The guitar is shrieking like something is stripping the life from it, the singer is howling their head clean off and beneath it all the drums and the bass are locked down in that endless, timeless groove…

When a fade is put on the end of a song it's meant to give the listener the impression that the song they're hearing will go on forever. This lack of resolution can be far more satisfying and ring truer than any resounding final crunch ever could. But usually a fade is just put on the end of a song to mask the fact that the band could never think of a proper ending. Or when a solid piece of work had started to fizzle and fall apart near the finish, the fade saved the piece its final dignity. Preserved it at its peak instead of revealing the disappointing and ordinary reality of the mess it actually amounted to.

But sometimes a fade could be the most honest ending there was. Because some things had no resolution. At least none we'd ever have the ability to listen through to the end. But we tried, didn't we? Every time, to hear a bit more before slipping back into the silence.

I played along, learning my part as I wrote it.

Acknowledgments:

Gratitude for the following foxy folks:
Garrett Cook, for asking me to write something.
Erin McGrath and Dan Cleri for reading what I wrote.
and Ross Lockhart, for telling me to write some more of it.

WINNER OF THE BRAM STOKER AWARD FOR SUPERIOR ACHIEVEMENT IN A NOVEL.

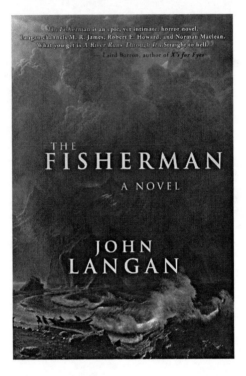

THE FISHERMAN is an epic, yet intimate, horror novel. Langan channels M. R. James, Robert E. Howard, and Norman Maclean. What you get is *A River Runs Through It*. Straight to hell.

—Laird Barron, author of *X's for Eyes*

THE FISHERMAN
A NOVEL
JOHN LANGAN

THIS IS HORROR NOVEL OF THE YEAR 2016

In upstate New York, in the woods around Woodstock, Dutchman's Creek flows out of the Ashokan Reservoir. Steep-banked, fast-moving, it offers the promise of fine fishing, and of something more, a possibility too fantastic to be true. When Abe and Dan, two widowers who have found solace in each other's company and a shared passion for fishing, hear rumors of the Creek, and what might be found there, the remedy to both their losses, they dismiss it as just another fish story. Soon, though, the men find themselves drawn into a tale as deep and old as the Reservoir. It's a tale of dark pacts, of long-buried secrets, and of a mysterious figure known as Der Fisher: the Fisherman. It will bring Abe and Dan face to face with all that they have lost, and with the price they must pay to regain it.

Trade Paperback, 282 pp, $16.99

ISBN-13: 978-1-939905-21-5

http://www.wordhorde.com

THIS IS HORROR SHORT STORY COLLECTION OF THE YEAR 2016

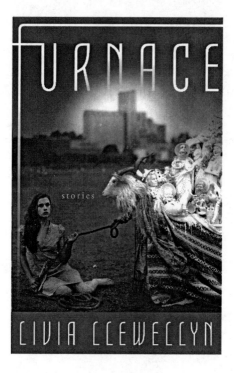

Horror fiction has long celebrated and explored the twin engines driving human existence. Call them what you like: Sex and Death, Love and Destruction, Temptation and Terror. While many may strive to reach the extremes, few authors manage to find the beauty that rests in the liminal space between these polar forces, the shuddering ecstasy encased within the shock. And then there's Livia Llewellyn, an author praised for her dark, stirring, evocative prose and disturbing, personal narratives.

Lush, layered, multifaceted, and elegant, the thirteen tales comprising *Furnace* showcase why Livia Llewellyn has been lauded by scholars and fans of weird fiction alike, and why she has been nominated multiple times for the Shirley Jackson Award and included in year's best anthologies. These are exquisite stories, of beauty and cruelty, of pleasure and pain, of hunger, and of sharp teeth sinking into tender flesh.

Format: Trade Paperback, 210 pp, $14.99

ISBN-13: 978-1-939905-17-8

http://www.wordhorde.com

Tony McMillen is the author of the novel *Nefarious Twit* and the graphic novel *Oblivion Suite*. He grew up mostly in Tucson, Arizona but now lives outside Boston with his wife and their invisible dog whom they call Invisipup. It's all so very damn precious. He writes, draws and plays the guitar but seldom all at the same time.

CPSIA information can be obtained
at www.ICGtesting.com
Printed in the USA
FFOW03n2016140617
36702FF

9 781939 905314